The F

Isaac Hooke

PUBLISHED BY:

Hooke Publishing
Copyright © 2013

IsaacHooke.com

Cover by:
Lars Von Lukas

CHAPTER ONE

Hoodwink stared at the sword that would take his head tonight.

The weapon was sealed away in a glass case for all to see, set there to remind the particular occupants of this section of the dungeon what their short futures held. It was a simple sword of dual-edged copper, with a blunt point. The jailer had taken the blade to the whetstone this very morning, and those edges gleamed in brutal anticipation. Scenes of agonized victims and delighted torturers etched its surface. The blade seemed rusted in places, perhaps from years of bloodletting. But copper didn't rust, so those dark brown marks had to be something else. Maybe stains from the headless men who'd shit themselves.

Hoodwink fingered the metallic collar around his neck. If he didn't have that bronze bitch on he would've broken down the dungeon cell with a bolt of lightning, taken the sword, and cut his way out of here in a storm of electrical glory.

The torchlight flickered and a draft of cold air kissed his neck. The touch brought him back to the present, where, outside the bars, Briar had been rattling on the whole time.

"Are you listening to me?" Briar said.

Hoodwink nodded. "Listening for all I'm worth, I am." Viewed through the long vertical bars embedded in the stone, Briar looked thinner somehow. Or maybe it was the rich, patterned silks the man had recently started wearing. Hoodwink recalled a time not too long ago when Briar had been the one in the dungeon, and Hoodwink the one on the outside. Briar sure wasn't dressed in silks back then.

"Look," Briar said. "I've got the whoremongers lined up. Clerks, witnesses, and so on and so forth. Damn shame the judge is a gol though. He would have been the first to bribe. Ah well, just have to pay someone else to take the fall. You know how it is. So many poor folk in this city. Do anything to support their families. Even die." He winked conspiratorially.

Hoodwink squeezed his fingers around the bars. "No."

Briar knotted his brow. "What did you say?"

"No." Hoodwink straightened his back, and stared the man down. "The only one who's taking the fall is me. You'll bribe no one, you won't." He had to protect her, no matter what.

"Oh please, don't you give me that holier-than-thou bullshit." Briar's face flushed scarlet. "This is hardly the time. It's your life we're talking about here."

"There's too many witnesses. They all saw me."

Briar threw up his hands. "They can be silenced. You know that. Each and every last one of them. And if they won't take the bribes..."

Hoodwink crossed his arms. "I don't want your help. Don't want no one's help. I don't. I'll take the blame for my actions." For *her* actions.

Briar shook his head and his jowls trembled. His collar was almost buried in the folds of neck fat.

"You've gone mad then, haven't ye?" Those eyes widened in mock surprise. "He's gone mad."

Hoodwink nodded toward Briar's throat. "You really ought to get that resized sometime."

"What," Briar said. "The bronze bitch?"

"No. Your neck." Normally he wouldn't insult Briar like that, but he just wanted him to go.

The simple-looking jailer came up. He wore black pants and a black vest over a white shirt. The middle of the shirt was stamped with the blood palm of his profession. He looked like a real person, as most gols did. Sometimes when you talked to gols you could almost believe they *were* real, if you kept things light, superficial. But engage in any deeper conversation and you routed them out. Gols, the mindless working class of the city-state.

The jailer nodded at Briar. "Visiting hours are up, krub." He wiped drool from his mouth with one sleeve. You would have never seen a gol doing something like that five years ago. The gols had really degenerated in the past few months.

"I heard you, gol," Briar said. "Jobe is it?"

The gol nodded. "My name is Jobe. Now get you to the surface, krub."

Briar smiled ironically, and glanced at Hoodwink. "Until later, then. Hopefully a few more hours in the asshole of the world will blast some sense into you."

Briar retrieved his fleece from the coat rack outside the cell, and ambled away down the torchlit tunnel. Hoodwink was suddenly aware of other eyes watching from the dark of nearby cells. Briar seemed oblivious, concerned only with moving his bulk up the tunnel. The man paused beside the display case that held the sword, and he shook his head, muttering something.

"Briar," Hoodwink said.

The man looked back.

Hoodwink almost didn't ask. He didn't want the other prisoners to hear. He closed his eyes, and when he opened them again he said, "Say sorry to Cora for me."

Briar frowned and he turned away. In moments he was a featureless silhouette among the shadows.

Hoodwink felt the jailer's eyes on him.

"What are you looking at gol?" He pulled the neck of his jail-issue orange robe tight, covering his upper chest, which was blistered and red from the events of this morning.

Jobe didn't blink. "I am on guard duty, krub."

Hoodwink scrunched up his face. "Don't you have something better to do than stare at me all day?"

"I am on guard duty, krub." Spoken exactly the same way. Jobe unexpectedly clouted the bars with his baton.

Hoodwink leaped back.

Jobe broke into a stupid grin.

Hoodwink shook his head, and limped over to the cell's only mat. "Damn gols."

Not only was Hoodwink's chest badly burned, but he'd hurt his ankle something nasty this morning during the capture. He'd given the Gate guards quite the chase, that's for sure. If he hadn't stopped to roll in the snow and douse the flames on his person he might've made it.

Lying on the mat, he lifted one hand to his face. The guttering torches whipped shadows across his knuckles. He made a fist. He could almost feel the electricity within, the power that was shielded away by the collar at his neck, the bronze bitch.

The gols had bitched him when he was fifteen, just when he'd started to develop his powers, like all the other humans who came of age. Bitched for twenty years. He had tried so many different things to get that collar off over the years, but nothing had worked.

Maybe he just hadn't tried hard enough.

"Your trial is tonight?" Jobe pressed. "Ahead of the murderers? Rapists? What did you do?"

Hoodwink ignored the gol, who was *still* staring at him.

Jobe wiped a batch of slobber from his lips. "Tonight your head goes bounce-bounce."

Hoodwink blinked, and a smile flitted across his face.

They'd have to break through the collar to make his head go fucking bounce-bounce.

CHAPTER TWO

Hoodwink sat behind a desk at the front of the courthouse with his back to the stands. He was shivering from the cold and his own nervousness. The shackles around his hands rattled quietly. A subtle mist emerged from his nostrils with every exhale.

One word repeated again and again in his mind.

Lightning lightning lightning.

LIGHTNING.

Behind him, the courthouse was packed. He'd been stunned by the sheer number of people who'd turned out to watch his public trial and execution, people who'd come here despite the snowstorm that was brewing outside. He didn't think he was that important. And he wasn't. The fact was, he hadn't been to an execution in a long time, and he'd simply forgotten what a draw the bloodsport could be. It seemed somehow fitting that the last execution he'd attend would be his own.

He wondered how many friends of his were in the crowd, seeing him disgraced like this. Probably not many. The notice had been too short. Arrested in the morning, tried and executed in the evening. That was gol "efficiency" for you. Only the locals who'd heard the crier's announcement would be present. No, he had no friends here.

As for Briar, the fat merchant had returned a few hours ago, but Hoodwink had given him the same answer—Hoodwink would take the fall for this, no matter what. Briar reluctantly gave in, with a promise to attend the execution. However Hoodwink hadn't seen the man among the multitudes tonight. It was for the best, probably.

"This court has heard the witnesses." The judge wore an ermineskin cloak over a black gown stamped in the chest with the gavel of his profession. The long white curls of a wig spilled over his forehead and down his back. He was one of the most lucid gols Hoodwink had witnessed in months. "The evidence is overwhelming. You have been placed by multiple observers at the scene, and caught committing the most horrendous act of terrorism this city has known in years. What do you have to say to all of this, krub Hoodwink Cooper?"

That I'm glad, he thought. *So damn glad none of them saw her.*

Instead: "I'm guilty."

Murmurs rippled through the crowd.

The judge eyed him critically. "So you admit that you attacked the Forever Gate?"

"I thoroughly admit this, your honor."

"That you defied our most ancient and sacred law?" It was forbidden to lay so much as a hand on the Gate.

"Defied? Defiled might be a better word. Raped in the arse." Hoodwink shot the audience the biggest shit-eating grin he could manage. One old woman gasped.

The judge slammed his gavel onto the sounding block of his desk, and Hoodwinked jumped, actually jumped. That thud had a certain finality to it. An end of ends.

The judge leaned forward in his chair. "Do you admit to belonging to the terror organization known as the Users?"

"I do." He nodded toward the envelope on the desk in front of him. "You'll find a full confession in there. Along with names." All fake, of course. He didn't even know a single User. But he had to play this out to the end. He had to protect her, and he just wanted to get this over with as fast as possible. To hell with this sham of a trial.

The judge lifted an eyebrow. "Then I will pronounce sentence. For the attack on this city's most important asset, and for the countless gol lives lost, I sentence you to immediate death by beheading."

"Thank you your honor." Hoodwink gave the onlookers a flourishing bow.

"He's mad!" someone in the audience shouted.

Hoodwink cocked his head. "Mad? You're the collared. It's *you* who are mad!" If they didn't believe he belonged to the Users before, they would now. The Users were the biggest advocates of an uncollared society. At least their graffiti implied as much. The Users wanted everyone running around with lightning. Somehow, Hoodwink didn't think that was a good idea.

"You're collared too, User *terrorist*!" came the repartee from someone in the audience.

Two guards restrained him. As if he could run anywhere with his arms and legs shackled. Both guards had swords belted to their waists, and one guard was an obvious gol, with the sword-and-shield symbol stamped into his breastplate. The other was collared, and his plate was free of markings. That seemed an odd dichotomy to Hoodwink—to be collared and free at the same time.

Hoodwink decided to play up his terrorist role. He was rather enjoying this. He looked at the collared guard like a judge. "You'd help kill someone who only wants the same thing as you? Someone who wants to be free?"

The guard elbowed Hoodwink in the ribs. "Keep silent gutter scum!"

Hoodwink inhaled in pain. "That was uncalled for."

The guard jabbed him in the ribs a second time. Hoodwink bit down the pain, and kept quiet.

The outer door near the judge's desk abruptly flung open and three gols wheeled a guillotine in from the cold. Hoodwink's heart sank when he saw it. He had hoped the snowdrifts were too deep to convey the death device from its storehouse, and that the executioner's sword he'd seen in the dungeon would be favored instead. Flakes of snow followed the guillotine inside. Hoodwink shivered, and not from the cold.

One of the gols slammed the door, shutting out the storm, and then the trio wheeled the guillotine forward, bringing it between the judge's stand and Hoodwink.

The crowd broke into a chant. "Behead! Behead! Behead!"

As the guards escorted him to the guillotine, Hoodwink noticed the various scenes of decapitation imprinted on the blade. Severed heads with eyes and tongues sticking out in over-dramatization. Headless bodies pumping blood. The inscription brought a fresh shiver: "Through me pass the final Gate."

The guards forced Hoodwink to kneel. One of them stuffed a pillow under his knees. Funny, that they'd waste comfort on a man who'd soon know the ultimate discomfort. The gol lawmakers wanted to cast themselves as ethical. Beheading was quick and painless. And *comfortable*.

The guards jammed his neck into the circular notch of the lower panel, and secured the similarly-notched upper plank over his collar, completing the head-prison. So much for comfort—Hoodwink was bound fast beneath that blade, locked in a hole that offered no leeway.

"Behead! Behead! Behead!"

The bronze bitch was the only thing protecting him from the deadly steel. Except that was no protection at all. The guillotine could cut right through the collars in a single blow. Made them seem like the paper collars children folded for themselves in their games of adulthood. With the headman's sword, at least there was a chance that the first blow would merely cut *into* the collar, and maybe only graze the skin beneath. It usually took two or three strikes to actually reach the neck, even with a fully sharpened blade. Which was why the courts had replaced the sword, he supposed. The sword offered what only the condemned and the drunk had the courage to try—a chance at freedom. Face the beheader's blade, and hope to your maker that it took the collar off and not your entire head. Hoodwink had only ever seen one man survive it, fifteen years ago. The man in question had escaped in a flurry of lightning strikes, only to have the soldiers track him down and execute him on the street.

Hoodwink had stopped going to executions after that.

At least that man had had a chance at survival, though. Hoodwink wouldn't get the same chance—the cold steel of this machine that assembly-lined death made sure of that. Lift the blade. Flick the lever. Chop off the head. He felt sick to his stomach. Good thing he hadn't eaten all day. It wouldn't do to sick up in front of all these people.

For her, he did this for her.

But would it be enough?

"Behead! Behead! Behead!"

The executioner approached from the front. He was a fat gol, but not as stout as Briar. A black hood covered his face. Wouldn't want to splash head blood on his features now would he? A long black apron hung around his neck, secured at the waist, just like a butcher's. That's what he was after all. A man-butcher. The red sword of his profession was proudly stamped into the apron.

Hoodwink cursed the gol, but he couldn't hear his own voice above the crowd. He noted that the executioner carried the blunt-tipped, green-colored sword from the dungeon at his waist. A backup in case the guillotine failed? He had no idea. Hoodwink wished all of a sudden he hadn't stopped going to executions...

And then the gol sidled from view, moving off to where he could work the mechanisms of the guillotine. Hoodwink tried to crane his neck to look, but the head-prison held him firmly.

"Behead! Behead! Behead!"

The cries of the crowd crescendoed, only to abruptly cease as a collective breath was held.

Hoodwink heard nothing for long moments. Finally a distinct, malevolent CLICK sounded.

He felt the vibrations as the blade descended along the guides. The loud rasp of steel on steel consumed all else.

His life flashed before him. A childhood spent on the streets of Luckdown District. Puberty, and the years of swindling and wenching that had earned him his name. Then came the two weeks of power at fifteen years old, the two glorious weeks before the gols found and collared him. The collaring changed him, and he sobered up, attempted to earn an honest living. He almost succeeded.

But then the jewel that lit up his life was taken away.

She deserved so much better.

The blade struck.

CHAPTER THREE

The impact jolted his entire body. A dark veil descended over his vision. The basket rushing up to meet his head?

No.

He blinked a few times, clearing away the darkness. The collection basket remained where it was a pace below him.

The impossible had occurred.

His head was still attached to his body.

Beside him, the executioner grunted in surprise. A few gasps came from the audience.

Hoodwink felt his face grow hot. A weight like that of the entire world pressed on his neck. He felt vertebrae and tendons shift ever so slightly.

It was obvious the blade hadn't passed clean through the bronze bitch, but he couldn't tell if any part of his own neck was severed, because the entire area *throbbed*. He had the presence of mind to wiggle his toes, and that told him what he needed to know.

He heard the executioner straining beside him, and Hoodwink's neck jerked up and down within the head-prison as the executioner repeatedly yanked the pulley linked to the blade. There came a pause, and the executioner must have looked at the judge, because Hoodwink heard him say, "Well keep trying you fool."

Hoodwink's head jerked up and down more rapidly, and stars pocked his vision. The executioner set a heavy boot on Hoodwink's shoulder and pressed hard. It felt like Hoodwink's whole right side was caving in, while his neck bent the other way.

Finally the blade slid free with a loud rasp. Hoodwink heard the killing instrument slam into the top of the guillotine, and he felt the vibration as the blade began its second beheading attempt.

A tingle of power arose inside him, and time seemed to slow. It started as a spark, deep in his mind, a flicker of electricity that expanded outward and traveled down his neck, across his torso, into his arms and legs to the tips of his fingers and toes. The electricity pulsed through him in waves, a starving hound leashed before a helpless doe, waiting for its master to unleash its fury.

The bronze bitch had sprung a leak.

Hoodwink pushed against that leak and released the electrical energy held at bay for twenty years inside him.

The entire apparatus exploded away from him. Guillotine, shackles, collar, blade.

The courthouse erupted in screams as debris tore through the spectators. Hoodwink glanced at the nearest benches. The onlookers were bruised and bloodied. He tried not to look overly long. He'd already seen one man with a bloody stump in place of an arm, and another with a thick shard of wood protruding from his belly. Hoodwink didn't need to see more. He knew those images would haunt him enough. He hadn't meant to hurt anyone.

Beside him, the judge and nearby guards lay unmoving, bodies mangled and broken. The executioner himself was still standing, torso nailed gurgling to the judge's desk by the guillotine blade. Hoodwink felt no regret for these. They were gols. Not real people like the spectators.

The guards at the back of the courthouse— behind the wounded bystanders—were forcing their way forward through the mayhem. Hoodwink tried to draw more lightning, but couldn't. He was so out of practice, he'd mistakenly used all his charge in that opening gambit. It would be hours, maybe days, before he fully recharged.

He snatched up the judge's ermineskin cloak, grabbed the executioner's blunt-tipped sword, and made for the back door, the same door they'd carried the guillotine in from. The limp from this morning had worsened—a wooden fragment protruded from his leg, adding to the pain of his previously twisted ankle.

Hoodwink threw his weight into the door and burst into an all-out snowstorm.

The sudden cold took him aback but he forced himself onward. The frigid gale blinded him and brought tears to his eyes. He hardly recognized this for a city street. He could see maybe ten paces, no more. Snow drifts had buried everything, leaving only a blurry landscape of white mounds.

He had to find shelter, and soon. The wind clawed right through his jail-issue orange robe.

His limp actually improved out there. The cold numbed the pain, just as it numbed everything else. But he advanced no faster, because the snow swallowed his legs to the thighs.

He heard shouts behind him as guards emerged from the courthouse. Hoodwink ducked down an alleyway, visible as such only because of the concave notch the drifts made between houses, and he waded hurriedly through the snow.

He reached the alley's edge and peered around it. Through the whirling snow he saw the spectators fleeing from the front of the courthouse. Good.

He hid the sword in his robes and joined the crowd, just another spectator injured in what the criers would undoubtedly call a terrorist attack. He pulled the stolen ermineskin cloak tight, hoping it hid most of his jail-issue robes. There was a woman just ahead of him. She had a bloody stump for an arm.

"I'm sorry," he said quietly, though his voice wouldn't have carried above the wind.

He risked a backward glance. The guards had emerged from the alleyway, and were scanning the crowd through the snowstorm. One of them met his eye, and gave a shout.

Hoodwink cursed his luck, wondering how the gol could have possibly identified him at this distance. He shoved his way through the crowd, limping as fast as he was able.

"This way!" An old man grabbed his hand. "I can help you!"

Hoodwink had scarce few friends right about now, and he could definitely use all the help he could get, so he let the old man lead him through the blowing snow. He felt the electricity slowly seeping back, fanning that spark deep in his mind. But it was a gradual seeping. Too gradual. A snail crossed a city street faster. It'd be another day or two before he returned to full strength.

He glanced over his shoulder. The wind whipped the veil of falling snow aside, and he caught a glimpse of the guards. They were closing the gap, and fast. Worse, more had joined the chase from a nearby barracks.

The crowd thinned, and soon the only thing between the guards and Hoodwink were the snowdrifts, and the blizzard. He pushed on, letting the old man drag him forward. Hoodwink limped for all he was worth. He truly did. But it was useless. The crunch of those pursuing boots kept getting louder.

"Leave me, old man." Hoodwink pushed the old man away. He didn't want someone else to get hurt because of him.

He turned to face his pursuers and tried to tap into his powers, but he couldn't even muster a spark.

It looked like the entire city guard had joined in the chase. The street was full of them, four ranks thick. Most were gol, but there were a few collared among them. Every sword was drawn.

Hoodwink raised his palms in surrender, wondering if they'd execute him on the spot.

CHAPTER FOUR

The guards slowed as they neared, perhaps suspecting a trap.

Hoodwink smiled, standing there on that street where he'd probably die. He kept his arms raised in surrender.

The closest guard—their leader?—was a gol with nasty cuts on one eye. The broken guillotine had mangled his face pretty good. No man could function with a face like that, not without some serious healing. But this was a gol, not a man, Hoodwink had to remind himself.

The guard stopped a full three paces away, and lifted a hand to halt the others behind him. The snow whirled between Hoodwink and the gol as the storm raged on.

"Well, get on with it Bleeding Eye!" Hoodwink said into the silence that followed this unexpected standoff. "Kill me." In answer came only the howl of the wind.

Hoodwink noticed a glow coming from his own leg. When he glanced down, he saw that the light came from the drops of blood trickling into the snow from his lacerated calf.

Drops of blood that glowed blue.

Hoodwink swallowed a rising panic. He'd accessed powers he hadn't used in ages. Forbidden powers. Who knew what the side effects were? He was dying, that much was certain.

He looked at the men again, and saw the uncertainty written on those faces. Not quite fright.

No, you couldn't frighten gols. But indecision, yes.

Perhaps he could use their indecision against them.

He was dead anyway.

He had nothing to lose.

Hoodwink took a menacing step forward. "The whole lot of you have five seconds before I explode you all. You think the guillotine was something? Just wait till I reduce you to cinders." That wasn't possible, of course, given how low his charge was. But the gols couldn't know. Nor even the human guards among them. Who could say what a murderous uncollared adult could do? They'd certainly heard the same stories as him. Stories about uncollared men ripping others apart with a look. Maybe they'd even faced some of those men. "Five seconds. Drop your swords and run. Five."

"Four."

"Three."

"Two."

They ran. All it took was Bleeding Eye turning his tail and the rest of them broke ranks. It was a complete route. Some slipped in their hurry to be away from there, and fell into the drifts. But they always got up again and, with a frantic looks back, ran on.

Hoodwink heard a strange sizzling.

He turned around, and realized it wasn't him who the gols were afraid of, but the banshee covered in writhing sparks of blue electricity behind him.

The banshee noticed his gaze and instantly

the electricity went out, leaving the old man in its place.

"You have lightning too." Hoodwink stared at the old man for a moment, but then his weariness finally caught up with him and he collapsed.

The old man helped him to his feet and braced him with one shoulder. Hoodwink was too drained to protest. The loss of blood was getting to him. He felt numb all over, but mostly in his hands and feet. Frostbite, undoubtedly.

"Who are you?" Hoodwink said.

The old man smiled indulgently, revealing a mouth as toothless as a street brawler's. "You'll know everything soon enough." The old man raised a hand sparking with electricity. Hoodwink recoiled, but the man clasped his palm and Hoodwink felt a surge of energy pass between them. "Feel better?"

Hoodwink nodded. He felt a little refreshed, and his extremities seemed less numb, though the old man still had to brace him with one arm as he led Hoodwink through the snowstorm. The conditions were becoming near whiteout, and the visibility certainly wasn't helped by the late hour. He let the surprisingly strong old man carry him onward, and the moments passed in a blur of snow drifts and weariness.

Hoodwink's gaze was drawn by movement to his left. He saw a bumblebee in the blizzard. The snowflakes parted to either side of the insect as if there were some invisible force emanating from the bee. It buzzed right up to Hoodwink's face and hovered there, a handspan from his nose, the flakes falling umbrellalike around it. Then it buzzed away.

Hoodwink was hallucinating from the blood loss obviously. He had likely imagined all of this. The blue blood. The old man's turn as an electrical banshee. But how did he escape the guards then?

Finally the old man paused before a flimsy door set into a cabin three times larger than its neighbors. The snow had piled up past the roof, and it was only through the diligent shoveling of whoever lived here that the door was even accessible. Hoodwink wasn't sure exactly where he was, but he was in no condition to resist as the old man dragged him inside.

"Helluva storm," the old man said as he shut the door behind them. He had to throw his weight into the wood to get the thing to close completely. "The prophets promised it would be an age of ice. Damn them for being right."

Hoodwink stood hunched in a cozy lobby. He was immediately attracted to the fireplace with its set of four ladderback chairs, where he plunked himself down. He was too weak to warm his hands over the coals, and he surveyed the room through half-closed lids. The windows were all frosted up, of course. An unmanned service desk lay near the fireplace. On the other side, the room opened into a hallway where the rooms were numbered.

"What is—" Hoodwink said, fighting off the sleep. "Where are—"

"Just a simple inn, laddy." The old man grabbed a poker from beside the fireplace and stoked the flames. "Let me apply a healing shard."

"A shard." It was illegal to carry one,

because to activate a shard required a User's power. Hoodwink smiled grimly. "Of course you have a shard."

The old man ripped open the hem of Hoodwink's jail-issue robe and slid the boot off. The pain roused Hoodwink somewhat. "Name's Alan. Alan Dooran. Friends call me Al."

Hoodwink glanced down to see a gory scene that nearly made him vomit. It hadn't looked so bad before, with the robe covering it, but now? A black sliver of bone jutted from the front of his calf alongside the wooden fragment, and the entire area had swollen the size of a melon. Blue blood drenched the entire lower leg. *Blue.* So he hadn't been hallucinating.

Well, the blood had stopped dripping, at least.

"Got yourself a nice piece of wood in your leg." Al grasped the wooden fragment and braced his boot on the top of Hoodwink's toes. "Better grip yourself tight."

"Wait," Hoodwink said. "Why is it blue?"

"Got no charge left," Al said nonchalantly.

The old man pulled the fragment.

Hoodwink struggled to stay in the chair as fresh spurts of pain flared in his calf. Stars exploded across his vision from the sheer agony of it, and when the wood broke free in a fountain of gore he cried out in pain.

The blood gushed from him in blue spurts.

"Looks like it hit a major artery." Al reached for the poker, and applied the sizzling end to Hoodwink's calf.

Teeth-grinding pain brought more stars to his vision, and Hoodwink felt his hold on consciousness grow tenuous. The burning didn't seem to do anything, and the blood gushed from him worse than ever.

He was barely aware as Al reached into his cloak and pulled out a crystalline creature that resembled a starfish.

The healing shard.

Al applied the creature to Hoodwink's calf. This thing, the shard, felt extremely cold against the hot pain of the wound, and Hoodwink gasped. Al released electricity into the shard, and the creature began melting into Hoodwink's skin. As it did so the melon-sized lump shrunk until both wound and creature were gone.

Hoodwink blinked away the nausea, and bent over to examine the wound. Not a trace of the injury remained. Even his twisted ankle further down felt a little better—he could revolve the foot with less pain.

"Careful," Al said. "You've lost a lot of blood."

Hoodwink stared at the blue puddle on the floor. "You're a User." He shouldn't have spoken, because he felt a fresh wave of nausea. He sat himself back in the chair. It was like he'd just run a marathon. His face was flushed, and he was panting. He shook his head, tried to clear his mind. His fingers had begun to burn now that they were thawing out. His toes fared just as badly.

"I am," Al said.

Hoodwink's gaze fell to the man's neck. "But

you wear a collar."

That smile widened. "Obviously ain't a real bronze bitch. Have to wear something to keep the gols at bay."

"Why did you save me, old man?"

Al straightened, as if offended. "The same reason I'd save any other innocent human being, of course. Because it's the right thing to do. And I ain't so old. Thirty-four, by my reckoning. Younger than you."

He looked closer to eighty-four, but Hoodwink didn't comment. Something else Al said had caught his attention. "You called me innocent."

"I did. I've something to show you." Al hoisted him to his feet, and helped him across the lobby. He led Hoodwink into the frigid hallway, where the candles burned low. Those carpets were grungy, the walls smeared in fingerprints. The rooms started at 2000, and increased sequentially. 2001, 2002, 2007, 2012,

Al stopped beside the one labeled 2013.

The old man lifted an eyebrow. "Ready?"

Hoodwink sighed. "No. But I have a feeling you'll make me go inside anyway."

Al smiled widely. "Smart boy."

He opened the door. Seven people were seated on ladderbacks in a circle, hands folded in their laps. They all turned their heads toward the doorway.

"Welcome to the secret society of the Users," Al said.

But Hoodwink hardly heard.

She was here.

CHAPTER FIVE

Hoodwink quickly shot a hand against the doorframe. It was all he could do to hold himself up.

There she was, the woman he'd given up everything for.

She regarded him uncertainly. "You."

He shoved the old man away, and lunged forward, step, by step. He felt certain his legs would give out on him at any moment.

When he reached her, his legs at last stopped working, and he fell to his knees. He covered his face in his hands. "Forgive me."

Al came up beside him. "You know her?"

Hoodwink didn't look up. "Of course I know her. She's my daughter."

He felt hesitant fingers rest on his head. Hers. "I'd wondered who my real father was," she said.

"Yolinda." He looked up at her, and he couldn't help the tears.

"I'm Ari now," she said, and she held his palm in hers. She looked older than he remembered her. Much older. It had only been six months, but she seemed to have aged at least ten years.

"Is this the man who interrupted you?" A rasping voice came from somewhere else in the circle.

"It is," Ari said.

Hoodwink looked from her, not caring who saw the emotion written all over his face, and he let his gaze pass from person to person.

So these were the legendary Users, those who had broken free of their collars and defied the gols. They looked ordinary enough. Unlike his daughter, they were all old, well into their eighties and nineties.

Al lifted Hoodwink into an empty chair beside his daughter, and pulled another chair up beside him.

"This is Hoodwink Cooper, everyone," Al said.

"Why did you interfere?" That rasping voice again. It belonged to an old barrel of a man with a pinched face that would've put the performers of the macabre circus to shame. He had intelligent eyes though, and spoke confidently.

"That's Marx by the way," Al said. "Though we call him Karl sometimes. Karl Blacksmith."

"I don't smith no more," Marx said. "Now answer the question."

Al whispered in his ear, "He's our torturer."

"She's my daughter, she is," Hoodwink said. "And I've passed her on the way to work every day since mayor Jeremy revised her. Every day, when she went out on her morning run. I guess I hoped she'd remember me. But she never returned my gaze, not once. Until this morning. She seemed so scared. Her eyes were huge, like she was calling out for help. So I followed her, I did. Watched as she waited by the Forever Gate. Watched as she dropped her satchel in the snow by the wall. I didn't know she was waiting for the street to clear. I didn't know she did it on purpose. I didn't know it was a bomb.

"So when she walked away, leaving it behind, I ran and picked it up from the snow, and that's when the gate guards grabbed me. They opened the satchel, accused me of terrorism. I broke away, and ran. That's when it went off." Hoodwink shook his head, looking at her. "I would have never thought she was capable of something like that. My own flesh and blood. Bombing the Gate? Never. But it's my fault. I shouldn't have let Jeremy have her those six months ago."

"It's no one's *fault*." Ari met his eyes steadily. The old Yolinda wouldn't have done that. Met his gaze, that is. She would've stared at the floor rather than face the full intensity of his wrath, or in this case, his disappointment. "No human beings died in the explosion. There were only gol casualties."

"Did Jeremy put you up to it?" Hoodwink asked her.

"Jeremy's powerful, I'll give him that." It was Marx who answered. "But no, Jeremy didn't order the bomb. The man's the *mayor*. He suckles the teat of the gols. He wouldn't dare risk something like this. No. *We* ordered Ari to place the bomb."

"You." Hoodwink spoke the word tonelessly. He glanced at Ari. "How did you get mixed up with these Users?"

It was Marx who answered. "When Mayor Jeremy had her revised, we sought her out. Her connections gave us access to the raw materials we needed to make the bomb."

"I for one didn't know she was revised." This from an old lady dressed in quilts who could have been Hoodwink's grandma. She held two knitting needles, with a spool of yarn in her lap. She seemed to be knitting the very same quilt that she wore.

"That's because you never pay attention at the meetings," Al said. "Ari refused to marry the mayor. So Jeremy had her personality *revised*."

Hoodwink shook his head. There was more to it than that, but he wasn't about to volunteer information to these Users.

"You poor dear." The old lady's eyebrows drooped. "Did it hurt?"

Ari smiled stiffly. "I don't remember."

"That's Vax by the way," Al said, nodding at the quilt lady. "You'll like her. Used to be a man."

The old lady sniffed, and returned to her knitting.

Hoodwink pressed his lips together. "Jeremy should have had me revised too. Should've made me forget I ever had a daughter. Spared me the pain."

Ari rested a hand in his. He wanted to shake it off, but she *was* his daughter. At least, she used to be. Even if she didn't remember.

A thought occurred to him, and he regarded Al suspiciously. "Why did you bring me here?"

Al looked across the seated old men and women to a frail elderly pauper dressed in rags who held a cane in palsied hands. The pauper kept his eyes forward, not looking at anyone else, maybe *not able* to look at anyone else, staring at some distant point on the wall.

"There is an old saying," the frail pauper said. "The truth, to the overwhelming majority of mankind, is indistinguishable from a headache."

"That's Leader," Al whispered.

Hoodwink studied the shabby-looking man. "*Leader*?"

"Aye, he leads us."

Leader focused his attention on Hoodwink suddenly, and those eyes held him in a grip quite unlike anything he'd ever experienced before. Hoodwink felt naked beneath those eyes, as though this man could see through all masks and pretenses and read the true nature of anyone. Hoodwink couldn't look away, though he sorely wanted to.

Leader broke the grip, and resumed his observation of the wall. There was nothing there that Hoodwink could see, except worn, curling wallpaper.

"I'm twenty-nine years old," Leader said.

"Thirty-nine here," Vax volunteered.

"Forty-two." Karl Marx.

And so the company rattled off their ages. No one present was over forty-five, though they all looked eighty or more. All save Ari.

"It's the price we pay for vitra," Leader said. "When the gols tell us that they collar us for our own protection, they mean it. Without the collar, the electrical current flows freely through our bodies, and ages us. Rapidly."

Hoodwink studied the man uncertainly.

"That is one truth." Leader nodded to himself. "Do you feel the better for knowing it?"

Hoodwink rubbed his hands together. "I never asked for the truth." He stopped the gesture. It was too much like washing his hands. Of the truth.

"But that's what you'll get when you're with us. The truth. Or a version of it, anyway." Leader gripped his cane tightly, and for a moment Hoodwink thought he was going to stand. But Leader merely shifted in his seat. "Something is wrong with the gols. They have been distracted lately. The gol banker giving out a thousand more drachmae than he should. The gol lutist forgetting his notes halfway through the ballad. The gol butcher misjudging his swing, and cutting off his own hand. The gol executioner, *forgetting to sharpen the guillotine blade*. I can cite examples from across the city. Then there's that blank, slobbering look so many of them have developed. It's as if they've contracted a plague of the mind."

"But the gols can't get sick," Hoodwink said.

Leader nodded. "So we have been taught. Perhaps they are under an attack of some sort, in the world beyond the Gate where they reside simultaneously to our own. The Outside."

Hoodwink rubbed his arms together, feeling suddenly cold. "I don't know what you're talking about. Residing simultaneously? And the Outside is dead. Everyone knows that."

Leader arched his eyebrows. "Indeed?"

"And if there really were an attack on the gols," Hoodwink said. "Would that be such a bad thing? I say let them be wiped out. A world without gols is a better world."

Leader smiled. "We blame them for imposing upon our freedoms, for collaring us, for confining us to the cities, it's true. And they hunt us, the uncollared. The Users. We all hate them, with passion. But at their core, they service us. You do realize this don't you? It's a love-hate relationship. Without the infrastructure they provide, civilization as we know it would collapse. We'd fall back into the dark ages, quite literally, and we'd all freeze to death."

Hoodwink wouldn't back down. "And we're not in the dark ages already?"

Leader opened his mouth, but he had no answer to that.

Hoodwink pressed his attack. "Why did you make Ari bomb the Forever Gate?"

"She was merely trying to open a path to the Outside," Leader said. "We want to help the gols with what ails them, you see."

"Help the gols." Hoodwink stood. "I've just about heard enough. You go and enjoy helping your gols." Hoodwink held out a hand to his daughter. "Come on Ari, let's go. You don't need these people ordering you around."

She didn't move.

Hoodwink heard a low buzzing. He glanced around the circle. The elderly men and women had raised their hands, and electricity flowed between them, from fingertip to fingertip.

"Please, Hoodwink, sit down." Leader said. "Please."

Hoodwink lifted his palms in surrender, and sat back down. He was relieved when the electrical flows ceased.

"Your daughter is the one who planned the Gate attack." Leader smiled that distant smile, and his eyes locked on Hoodwink. "Do you want to know the truth? What lies beyond the Forever Gate?"

Hoodwink couldn't answer. That gaze overwhelmed him.

Leader was still smiling when he looked away. "It is a land quite unlike any we have ever known. It— well, it is the land where the gols reside in actuality. As different from this world as the bottom of the ocean is from the top of the sky. In the city, none of the gols can even comprehend our offer of help. It's beyond their programming. We can't break past the generic response loops. But beyond the Gate, they will listen to us. They *will*."

Hoodwink sat back. "How do you know they'll even want your help?"

Leader sighed. "We don't. But we must try."

"Okay." Hoodwink glanced from face to face. The expressions were grim, and some of those present glowered at him. "You're forgetting one small thing. You have to *go through the Gate* Ari couldn't even make a dent in it with that bomb of hers. So as far as I'm concerned, this discussion is pointless. And I still don't know why you're even telling me all this."

"The bomb was only a hope we'd entertained. To create a passage for us all. But there is another way." Leader was silent a moment. He stared at that peeling wallpaper, and the guttering wall candles flicked shadows across his face. "It is a dangerous path, too perilous for most of us. A path only the strong and hale among us can take."

Leader's eyes found Hoodwink, and then shifted to Ari, at his side.

Hoodwink realized what the man implied, and he stood. "Ari's not doing it."

"You're not my father anymore, remember that," Ari said quietly.

Hoodwink didn't look at her. "Whatever you planned for her, I will do. Send me in her place."

Leader nodded to himself. "This is what I want, too. Ari must stay here. Her connections to the mayor are too important. Someone else must go. Someone newly uncollared, yet still strong in body. But you should know, no one we've ever sent beyond the Gate has returned."

"I don't need you to save me," Ari said.

"I'll do it," Hoodwink insisted. He wasn't going to lose her again.

Leader nodded solemnly. "If there's anyone you want to say good-bye to, anyone at all, now's the time. Because as I said, no one's ever come back."

Hoodwink glanced at Ari. "I plan to be the first."

CHAPTER SIX

Hoodwink strode through the wintry streets of the city that birthed him.

He'd spent the night in exhausted sleep at the inn. By morning, the snowstorm had let up, allowing the sun to shine weakly in the cold sky. The Users had given him leave to make his good-byes, and so he left. Ari had joined him. He wasn't sure if she came for the company, or to act as his keeper. He didn't mind either way.

He made his way across one of the richer quarters of the city. Even here the gols were still shoveling the snow from the recent storm. A few shopkeepers had pitched in, piling the snow into deep drifts beside their walls, and for the most part the street was clear. Many of the shops had reopened, since most of the buildings also served as homes for the owners—to open up was as simple as unlocking the front door and flipping the sign. Almost all of the buildings were single-story dwellings of gray rock, though there were a few two-stories among them.

A few buyers were already out, dressed in heavy cloaks, moving between the shops. Pretty-faced hostesses in fur coats beckoned customers to eat at their restaurants. Smoky-voiced doormen announced post-snowstorm deals at their taverns.

Hoodwink tried to soak-up as much of it as he could. This might be the last time he saw all of this. Leader had given him only an hour to get his affairs in order, and then Hoodwink was to seek him out on Forever Street. One hour.

I'm going to miss this place, he thought. And yet he felt content, because Ari walked at his side. Ari, the daughter he had thought lost to him. The daughter he would have sacrificed everything for. *At his side*. Even if he only had an hour to live, it was all worth it, because she was here.

"I'd given up, you know," Hoodwink said into the dragging silence between them.

Ari glanced at him distractedly. "On what, Hoodwink?"

"On you. On myself. I didn't, well, I guess you could say, when you left, my world ended. It really did. I wasn't myself anymore. And now you're back and everything's okay again."

"I'm not sure what to say to that." Ari crossed her arms. "Sounds like I've some pretty big shoes to fill."

"You don't have to say anything." Hoodwink smiled. "You're filling them just by being here, you are."

Ari declined an invitation to eat at a restaurant from a well-groomed host. When the host made the same offer to Hoodwink, he immediately raised his hands. "Not me young man, I'm poor." The man smirked, and then turned to accost the next passer-by.

"You know," Hoodwink told Ari as they continued on. "I've always felt a little uncomfortable in the richer parts of the city like this. It's not so much I can't afford to shop in these places—if I really wanted to, I could come here and blow a few month's wages—but it's more the beggars looking for handouts that bother me." He nodded at a dirty-faced mendicant perched between one of the storefronts. He and Ari had passed many such men already, and he gave each and every one of them a wide berth, including this latest. "They remind me of the ashes of poverty I've risen up from. Maybe it's a reminder I need now and again to keep myself sharp, knowing that it can be something as small as a month's pay that separates the haves from the have-nots."

Ari was smiling, and seemed to be struggling to suppress a giggle.

Hoodwink frowned. "I was being serious. You find something funny?"

"Nothing," she said. "It's just, I've always wondered what you'd be like. My real father. Not the one from my revised memories, but the father I hoped I'd one day meet. And here you are, eccentricities and all."

Hoodwink watched her uncertainly. "Am I everything you expected me to be?"

Ari shook her head. "I'm not sure yet. I just, well, all of this is new to me."

"It's new to me too, Yolin— Ari. The past doesn't matter. The memories you have, they don't matter. What we have here, right now, this is the truth. This is what matters. I never want to leave your life again."

Ari tightened her crossed arms, shivering. "And yet you'll soon do just that."

"But I will return, I promised this already." Hoodwink rubbed the tip of his mustache, a nervous habit of his. "And I'm not one to break promises."

Ari didn't seem convinced. "Even if it's a promise you can't keep?"

"I never make a promise I can't keep."

She laughed, shaking her head. It was the same laugh he remembered. "Are you always this confident?"

Hoodwink grinned widely. "Only around my daughter."

Ahead, a street busker strummed a mandolin. Hoodwink began edging sideways, acting as if the man carried the plague. But Ari stayed true to her course, and stopped—actually stopped—to listen to the man play and sing his sad song. When he was done, Ari dropped three fat coins into his hat, and the man thanked her profusely.

Hoodwink reached into his pocket and guiltily left a small silver coin, all he had on his person.

"You're better than me, Ari," Hoodwink said as they moved on. "That's why I'm doing this, you know. The world needs you. But me, I'm just, well, I'm just a middle-aged, miserly barrel-maker. Not young and generous of heart like you."

Ari seemed troubled. "Generous, maybe, but I won't be young for long unfortunately."

"Then leave the Users. You don't owe them a thing. You have your whole life ahead of you."

She shook her head. "I can't, Hoodwink. First of all, I'd have to give up vitra. You've tasted it. The power, the sense that you're truly alive. That's not something you can let go off easily." Hoodwink couldn't disagree there. "And second of all, for once in my life I feel like I belong to something. Feel like I'm making a difference. We can help the world as Users. I have to stay. You must see that."

"What I do see," Hoodwink said. "Is that you've inherited my famous stubbornness. A part of the old Yolinda is still inside you after all."

Ari pressed her lips together, and she looked away. "I'd like to think so."

"Oh, I know so." Hoodwink rested a hand on her shoulder. "You stopped for the busker. You could've given him the coins and walked on. But you stopped to listen. Why?"

"I don't honestly know." She tapped her chin with a finger. "I've always liked music, I suppose. And that song he was singing, well, it got to me, you know? I felt it deep inside."

"Your mom always wanted to be a singer. She used to sing to you, every night before bed."

Ari leaped over a slushy area of ground in front of a tavern. "The mother of my revised memories hates singers, and anyone who wants to sing. She told me that singing was daft, and music was for the birds."

"Which is the furthest thing from your actual mother," Hoodwink said. "Do you see? It proves that the old Yolinda is still in there somewhere."

Ari's lips twitched in irony. "How do you know I didn't stop and listen to the busker just to spite the memory of my false, music-hating mother?"

Hoodwink couldn't help but smile. There was definitely some of the old Yolinda left in her.

The two walked in silence for a time. He felt

the fake collar the blacksmith Karl had given him, its bronze pressing against his throat. The sham seemed to be working so far. No one paid him or Ari any heed. Earlier he'd even passed a group of gol soldiers, and none had even spared him a glance. He supposed it helped that his prison-issue robes were gone, replaced by an inconspicuous dun coat. He also wore mittens and a cloak—an outfit that was at least somewhat appropriate for this quarter.

It was close to mid-morning, and the slightly warmer temperatures encouraged frigid pockets of mist. As Hoodwink and Ari stepped into one such pocket, Hoodwink's thoughts seemed to cloud as well. He and Ari had to weave left and right to avoid the murky shapes of passers-by.

His mind wandered, and he thought of the Forever Gate. He was going to cross it and stare death in the face a little under an hour from now. Incredible.

"I sometimes have this recurring dream." Hoodwink felt freer to talk now that his face was half-obscured in mist, just as if this moment were itself a dream. "In it, I'm always in a faraway place. In a land nothing like this one. A land long drowned. In the dream, I'm bodiless, and I see in all directions at once. It terrifies me."

Ari remained silence. There was only the sound of their footsteps on the shoveled cobblestone, and the footfalls of the ghostly passers-by.

"I lay awake afterwards," he continued. "And wonder: Is that where I will go when I die?

Will I live forever in that faraway land? And more importantly, do I *want* to live forever there? Spending an eternity as some bodiless entity, remembering what I once was, and never able to return doesn't have much appeal."

Ari seemed to stiffen beside him. "Why are you telling me this?"

Hoodwink sighed. "I don't know. I guess I'm afraid of the Gate and what lies beyond it. Afraid of death. There's a reason why we have a Forever Gate. A reason why not even the gols will cross it. And your Users don't know half the truth of it either, though they pretend they do."

Ari sounded sad. "You don't have to do this Hoodwink. I never asked you to."

"I know Ari. But I *want* to do it. It has to be me. You know that."

The fog lifted as the two of them passed into Grassylane district, where the mansions of moderately successful merchants squatted behind fences of bronze and gates of iron. Despite the district's name, there was no grass here.

"You should come in," Hoodwink said. "And meet her."

Ari shook her head. "I think... I think it's better if you go alone. I'll meet you with Leader at the rendezvous. Good luck Hoodwink."

She gave him a quick hug and turned back.

Hoodwink watched her vanish into the mist, just as if she herself had only ever existed in a dream.

CHAPTER SEVEN

Hoodwink sat with chattering teeth in a plush chair in the sitting room, right where the maid had told him to. Those cold, travertine walls seemed to be closing in around him. He hated travertine. It was like ice in this weather, and the sitting room had no fireplace. But that was the style of the rich. And the rich so loved imitating the rich.

Well, at least the floor was carpeted. That helped retain some of the heat. Still, it wasn't for the cold that he was shivering. No, he worried what his reception would be. He hadn't come to this place in six months. And visiting now, after what happened yesterday morning... the maid's eyes had nearly bugged out of their head when she saw him at the door, and it was only with an effort that she managed to calm herself down after he'd forced his way in.

He was staring at a wall hanging of a strange underwater scene when Briar came into the foyer. The two exchanged how-are-yous and exuberant jolly-goods just as if Hoodwink wasn't a fugitive wanted for terrorism.

"You didn't come to my execution," Hoodwink said.

"Oh, you know how it is," Briar said casually, just as if the two of them were talking about some idle matter. "The life of a merchant. Always something to do: A client to visit, supplies to haul, money to count. Besides—" Briar palmed his chin and became very serious. "I didn't need to see you get killed, Hoodwink. I didn't need my last memory of you to be a body's worth of blood gushing from your headless corpse."

"Sure." Hoodwink quickly segued into the reason he'd come. "Is Cora home?"

"Cora? No, she's in Rhagnorak, training to be a singer. Didn't I tell you about her application?"

Rhagnorak. A city at least two portal hops away. You couldn't walk Outside between the cities, but you could travel to them by portal. "No." Hoodwink tried to hide his disappointment. "You never told me." At least she was finally achieving her dreams now, if that was true.

Briar slapped him on the knee. "You dirty rascal! You just can't leave my sister alone can you!" Briar seemed a little too jolly, like he was trying to hide something. Or was he just nervous that an escaped terrorist had called upon him?

"I'm going past the Gate, Briar," Hoodwink said. "I'm going Outside, I am."

Briar merely gaped at him. "Well that's... that's very nice. Good for you."

"I've met the Users."

"Really?" Briar wiped at his brow, visibly perspiring now. "Interesting. I've never been sure if they were just some rogue organization invented by the gols as a funnel for our hate. A political tool. Your little terrorist act caught the attention of the Users, did it? Terrorism attracts terrorists, I suppose."

Hoodwink held up his hand, extending one index finger. Sparks of electricity danced from it. Briar flinched.

"What are you hiding, Briar?" Hoodwink said.

"Well!" Briar stood. "Good luck to you in your adventures on the Outside and all. Tally-ho." He turned toward the hall, but was too late, it seemed, because Cora stood transfixed behind him.

"Cora darling," Briar said. "I told you to stay in your room."

She pushed past him.

"So it really is you." Cora stood over Hoodwink. "I knew Briar lied to me. He told me the maid had shooed off some beggar at our door. But then while I was lying on my bed, I heard your voice, and I thought, no, it can't be. Surely Hoodwink wouldn't come *here*, of all places. Surely Hoodwink wouldn't dare set foot in my brother's home. Not after what he did to me." Cora had never forgiven him for what happened to their daughter, and she never would, though she knew it wasn't his fault.

Hoodwink didn't meet her eye. "I've talked to our daughter, Cora. She's well. Doesn't remember us, of course."

"Can't you just leave her alone, Hood?" Cora said. "Can't you just leave *me* alone?"

He was going to say more about Ari, but there was something he wanted to mention first. "When Briar told me you went to Rhagnorak, I was so happy for you Cora. Happy that you're finally living your life again. I want you to succeed. I always have. You should really go. Make the application if you haven't. Be happy."

He risked meeting her gaze. Her face was

full of ire, and resentment.

"Happy?" She seemed to spit the word. "I can never be happy again. Not after..." She shook her head. "No, I'm not going to Rhagnorak. Happiness? I'm happy just to make it through to the next day. One morning at a time, that's the only way I can face life. Now, if you don't mind." She gestured toward the door.

Hoodwink didn't move. "Don't you want to hear what our daughter had to say?"

"It's not her anymore, Hoodwink. When are you going to get that in your head? She's lost to us."

"All right," he said. "All right. There's another reason I came."

"Please, say what you came to say then, and just go."

Hoodwink sighed. "As you wish. I came to say good-bye, I did. And, well, I've never stopped loving you, for what it's worth."

She smiled sardonically. "Not much. Good-bye then. Now go."

This wasn't quite going the way he'd expected. Not at all. She was trying to hurt him. Well, he could hurt her back so easily. *With all your brother's money, you couldn't save her*, he wanted to say. *Though you ran into his arms, begging him to take you in.* But no, he wasn't here to hurt her, and doing so wouldn't lessen his own feelings of guilt.

"There's something else," he said. "But before I say anything more, I want you to know, I'm not telling you this to hurt you." He swallowed nervously. "Our daughter was the one who planted the bomb at the Forever Gate."

Cora's lips twitched, but she said nothing.

"The Users put her up to it. She's one of them, now. They wanted her to cross to the Outside. They wanted her to talk to the gols out there."

"Stop it." Cora said. "Stop it. Stop it! Get out of here!"

He barreled on. It was important to him that she knew his sacrifice. "I wouldn't let her do it. The Users are sending me in her place. I'll probably die."

"Please," Cora said, covering her face. "Just go."

He hadn't wanted to hurt her, yet it appeared he'd done that very thing. He took a step forward. "Cora. I didn't mean—"

Briar hugged her, and turned her away from him. "Hoodwink..."

"I'm sorry," Hoodwink said, feeling terrible. Why did he always hurt those closest to him? He went to the front door.

Before he could open it, a harsh knock came from outside. "City watch! Open up!"

Hoodwink froze, and shot Briar an accusing glance.

"Sorry, Hood." Briar backed away, bringing Cora with him. "I really am. They've been watching my house since your escape."

The door thudded so heavily that it shook on its hinges. "Open up now or we'll break it down!"

"You bastard." The sparks flared on Hoodwink's knuckles. But it was just a show. He wasn't fully charged, not even close. He wouldn't be able to take on the city guard, not in his condition.

"You didn't say a word. How did they get to you? Yesterday you were begging to save my life."

Briar's chin quivered. "Yesterday you were collared. Innocent until proven guilty, and all that. Today you're a User fugitive. A terrorist. I had to give you up. Mayor Jeremy promised he'd have my hide if I harbored you."

"Jeremy." Hoodwink nearly spat the name. "Bad move, Briar. Very bad move. Because now *I'll* have your hide."

Hoodwink drew his green sword and Cora screamed. Hoodwink had wanted to scare Briar, not her, and when he saw the look of fear on his wife's face, a look that said "I don't even know who you are anymore," Hoodwink felt utter shame.

The knock came again, more frantic.

Hoodwink raced into the hall past Cora and Briar, making for the rear entrance. He heard Briar open the front door to the troops, heard the clank as the gols dashed onto the travertine floor behind him.

He swept through the kitchen toward the back door. The scullery maids screamed at the sight of his sword.

The back door abruptly flung open and reserve troops flooded in with swords raised.

CHAPTER EIGHT

Hoodwink backtracked through the kitchen and took the short staircase in the hall moments before the troops from the front converged on him. He climbed those stairs three at a time and came out at a lung-burning dash onto the second floor. Shouts came from behind as he sprinted across the deerskin carpet, toward the window that backed onto the rear alley. He leaped, and swung his sword to shatter the glass as he struck.

He was counting on the deep snow drifts in the alley outside to pad his fall, and he wasn't disappointed.

"Hey!" One of the sentries assigned to the back door outside spotted him.

Covered in snow, Hoodwink rolled to his feet and waded through the alleyway drifts, the shouts of pursuit harrying him on.

He stumbled over the windrow that blocked the end of the alleyway, and emerged onto the main street, thankful that the gols had shoveled this quarter of the city.

He ran for some time. Behind, the guards gave chase, harrying him on.

He veered onto Luckdown district and the path became bumpy with unshoveled snowpack.

Hoodwink nearly slipped more than once, though he had nails hammered point-first through the soles of his boots. The shouts grew closer. He glanced over his shoulder. The guards were only paces behind.

Hoodwink took a sharp right at Down Street. Too sharp. He slid right into a foodcart.

He scrambled to his feet—

Into the arms of a guard.

"Give 'er up, krub!" the gol said, tightening his arms around Hoodwink's chest. Others quickly approached—

Hoodwink angled the guard between himself and the bottom of Down Street, and then he hurled himself backward. He and the guard tumbled onto the sloped snowpack and gravity took over. The two slid down the steep hill, picking up speed by the moment. Bumps in the packed snow jolted the two continuously. The few street-goers gave the pair a wide berth, not wanting to join in that perilous slide.

The soldier tightened his grip during the descent, slowly crushing the air from Hoodwink's lungs. Hoodwink tried to pry that grip open, but it was like trying to take off one of the collars. He focused on the spark inside him instead. He wouldn't be able to generate much. He closed his eyes, and released a flare of electricity up and down his torso. The man's arms jolted away.

Handy, that.

Still sliding down, Hoodwink turned and gave the gol a good punch to the nose. Finally the road curved up to catch them, and the two slid to a halt. Hoodwink scrambled to his feet, kicked the gol in the belly for good measure, and raced on. About five seconds behind him, the four remaining soldiers slid to the bottom of the street and gave chase.

There was a market ahead, one that was

always crowded after snowstorms. Sure enough the throngs were packing it today. He hurried in among the crowds, weaving his way past peddlers, entertainers, and beggars. He quickly sat down beside a stand of skewered dog meat, lowered his head and extended his hand like the beggars he so feared, and waited.

The four guards jostled their way through the market. They passed almost right in front of him, oblivious to his presence.

The instant they had gone, Hoodwink stood up and hurried from the square.

He'd made it.

It wasn't long before he reached Forever Street, the road that lay in the shadow of the Gate. You could circle the entire city if you walked that street long enough. Beside it, the aptly-named wall that was the Forever Gate reached into the sky, the topmost edges lost in the clouds. The Forever Gate entombed the city, preventing all access to the Outside.

He passed the section where Ari had placed the bomb the day before. The area was blackened, but otherwise unharmed. One would have expected the gols to beef up their presence after an attack like that, but there actually seemed less gols along this portion of the wall today. There weren't enough of them to watch every section of the Gate every waking moment, Hoodwink supposed, especially when the wall was, by all indications, indestructible.

He soon met up with Leader. The ancient man observed the Forever Gate from the shade of a vendor who sold maps and miniature replicas of the city.

"Your goodbyes went well?" Leader asked, his breath misting. He stared off to the side in that way he had of not meeting one's eye.

"Splendid." Hoodwink picked up a replica of the city.

The vendor immediately stood up. "Touch and pay," the middle-aged woman said.

Hoodwink gingerly returned the replica.

Ari came up beside him and saved him from the woman by giving him a hug.

"How did it go?" Ari said. She carried two duffel bags, one big and one small, on each shoulder.

Hoodwink smiled sadly. "Cora says good-bye."

"You told her everything?"

He nodded.

"I'll seek her out," Ari said. "Let her know you spoke the truth."

"She knows." Hoodwink shook his head. "But don't go to her. It's probably better if she never sees you again."

Ari seemed about to contest him, but then she bit back whatever it was she was going to say.

Leader rested a palsied hand on his shoulder and finally turned that penetrating gaze on him. "Time wastes. Are you ready?"

Hoodwink shrugged. "As I'll ever be."

Ari handed the larger duffel bag to Hoodwink, and kept the smaller one for herself. Then he and Ari walked on either side of Leader, helping the haggard man through the streets. Leader verbally steered them down the byways to a secluded back alley.

The snow was never shoveled here, nor was it packed by the tread of passersby, so the three of them had to wade and dig through snow that was sometimes chest high. They reached a rusty iron gate that was nearly buried by the drifts, and Leader opened it with a key he'd brought along. The gate was like a portcullis, and they were able to slide it upward with some difficulty. Once through, Hoodwink saw that the alley offered secluded access to a portion of the Gate.

"Why didn't you put the bomb here?" he said.

Ari shook her head. "There'd be too much damage to the neighboring buildings. We didn't want any human casualties, remember?"

The three dug their way forward through the snow, until the sky-reaching wall consumed everything else. The Forever Gate. What looked like a flat, gray surface from far away was actually a craggy mountain of sheer, infinite stone. A silver rope dangled from the heights, and Hoodwink followed it with his eyes. He couldn't see where the rope anchored—it became lost in the coarse texture of the wall a mile or so up.

"You expect me to climb this?" Hoodwink pulled at the rope. He felt the echo of a distant vibration pass through the material. The sensation was eerie, like plucking the string of a giant lute.

"Think of it as a symbol." Leader gazed blankly up the wall. "Of the hurdles you've faced in this life. You have overcome them all to get to this point. Now you must overcome this last." Leader turned his eyes downward, to the snow drift piled against the wall. "We tried to dig under it at first. Like the sappers of yesteryear. That proved a mistake. The wall is buried in the ground at least as deep as it is high. And digging through frozen ground isn't a pleasant thing." He pursed his lips. "It was the time of our exploratory years. When we believed the Outside a sanctuary. A few of us came up with the rope idea. Erdus and Callus were the first to surmount the wall. They'd practiced for years, taught themselves the lost art of mountaineering. It was they who anchored the ropes. Good men. Their loss was irreplaceable." Leader's eyes drifted upward. "The climb will take around five hours. You'll find a new rope every half hour or so. There are ten in total. You've committed the address to memory?"

Hoodwink sighed. "John Baker, son of Arrold Baker, 18 Market Street." Though not a User, John was a close cousin of Leader. John assumed quite the risk by being their middle man. Hoodwink hoped the gols didn't use him to hunt the rest of the Users down. But Ari and the others were too smart to let that happen.

Leader motioned to the duffel bag slung over Hoodwink's shoulder, the one Ari had given him. "Put on the climbing gear."

Hoodwink slid the bag to the ground. He removed his cloak and handed it to Ari, and then he opened the bag and retrieved a balaclava. He slid the warm cloth down over his face, properly aligning the eyeholes so he could see. He was worried at first that he wouldn't have any air without holes for the nose and mouth, but he seemed to breathe fine through the balaclava's fabric. His breath did sound loud in his ears, though.

Next he swapped his thick mittens for the thinner climbing gloves contained in the bag.

"Gloves with leather palms for rope handling," Leader explained. "The tips can be folded back, and they become fingerless if you ever need a better grip. When you expose the fingers you'll have to expend charge to keep from getting frostbite, of course."

Hoodwink slid the top section of the gloves open, and sure enough the tips of his fingers were exposed. He slid the gloves closed again. He reached into the duffel bag and removed a thick jacket and extra layer of pants.

"Down jacket," Leader said as and Hoodwink slid the jacket over his fleece sweater and buttoned up the front. "One of the thickest jackets available. Made with the down feathers from the Eider ducks of the south. You'll be hot at first wearing that, but trust me, as you near the top of the Gate, you'll be glad you have it. The pants are down-stuffed as well. You'll have to leave your sword."

Hoodwink's fingers protectively clasped the hilt. "What if I need it?" His voice sounded muffled inside the balaclava.

Leader compressed his lips. "It'll only weight you down. Won't fit in the down pants anyway."

Ari stepped forward. "I'll give you my

dagger," she offered.

Hoodwink reluctantly unbuckled his sword and scabbard and gave it to Ari. He accepted her small dagger in exchange and stuffed it into an inner pocket of his jacket. Hoodwink slid the pants over his boots and up onto his existing woolen trousers, covering the dagger. He buttoned up the pants, and when he lowered his hands the jacket hem tumbled over his waist, ensuring that his midsection would remain warm during the climb.

Hoodwink retrieved the next item from the bag—a pair of goggles.

"Those are to protect your eyes from wind," Leader said. "Frozen corneas aren't a fun thing. You're familiar with frostbite? Well, when a frozen cornea thaws out, it's like a third degree burn in the eyes."

Hoodwink pulled the strap and gingerly lowered the goggles over his head. They fit securely over the eyeholes of the balaclava so that no portion of his face was now exposed. Although the periphery of his vision was blocked by the goggles, he could see well enough.

The last items in the bag were a pair of spiked metal frames a little larger than his palms, with leather straps on top. Hoodwink held them up curiously.

"Those are for your boots," Leader said. "Crampons, they're called. They give your feet purchase where there is none. You won't really need them until you reach the icy patches higher up. Still, they shouldn't wear down too badly against ordinary rock, and they'll be a hassle to put on midway the climb, so I suggest you strap them on now."

Hoodwink slipped the crampons over his boots. The metal spikes protruded from all sides of each boot, with two particularly long, mandible-like extensions at the fronts. He tightened the straps, fitting the crampons securely to his boots. When he stood, it felt like he walked on nails, and he had to extend his arms for balance.

The bag was now empty, and Hoodwink returned it to Ari. She stowed his cloak and sword inside, then slung it over her shoulder. She reached behind his head and raised the fur-lined hood of his jacket. She pulled the drawstrings, tightening the hood around his balaclava.

"You were damn right about it being hot," Hoodwink said, his voice sounding even more muffled now.

Ari handed him the second, smaller duffel bag she carried.

"In that one," Leader said. "You'll find the usual suspects. A water bladder. Probably will freeze solid higher up. A pee bottle. Probably won't need it. Salted meat. Probably won't be hungry. Couple of light ice axes. Oh, and the ever important rigged diary. Use it. Keep us updated."

The Users had either found the diaries or created them in years bygone—it wasn't made clear to Hoodwink. Whatever the case, the books came in pairs. When you wrote in one, your words appeared in the other no matter how far away you were.

Hoodwink secured the smaller duffel bag over his shoulder.

"You never told me," Hoodwink said. "Did

you give diaries to the others who went over this wall?"

Leader's palsy seemed to have gotten worse in the last few moments—his lips twitched and his eyes blinked spasmodically. Maybe he was just excited. Or nervous. "We did give them diaries, yes."

Hoodwink wanted the man to look at him, wanted to stare into those eyes and see what truths he could read there, but Leader didn't oblige.

"And what did you get back?" Hoodwink said.

A smile came to Leader's twitching lips. It reminded Hoodwink of a slithering snake. "The truth."

The old man was shaking all over now, and he removed one of his mittens and extended the palm toward Hoodwink. The start of a handshake.

Hoodwink accepted the palm.

A massive surge of current passed from Leader through Hoodwink's gloves and into his hand. Hoodwink couldn't move or break the grip. He could only stand there, just shaking spasmodically with Leader for long moments.

When the old man finally released him, both of them collapsed.

Viewing the world from where he lay sprawled in the snow, Hoodwink blinked a few times and then, feeling strangely full of energy, he scrambled to his feet.

The spark veritably flared inside him.

Leader had recharged him.

Ari helped Leader rise. The old man had

stopped twitching, and his face was deathly pale. His breath came in wheezes.

"Thank you," Hoodwink said.

Leader nodded slowly. "I have one last... gift for you." His voice sounded weak, and Hoodwink had to lean in closer to hear. "A word of caution, really. Once you reach the tenth rope, you're in the Death Zone. So high that there's a third less oxygen than down here. You'll feel utterly exhausted because of the thin air. You won't be able to think clearly. Nothing worse than being at the top of the world, balanced between life and death, and not being able to think. One thing is for certain—stay in the Death Zone too long, and you die."

"What are you saying?"

Leader smiled grimly. "Keep climbing. At the very top, you'll want to fall asleep. Truly, you will." The old man gazed into Hoodwink's eyes for the first time this meeting. There was a certain sternness to them. "Fall asleep and you die. Now go. Before you change your mind. And good luck."

Ari kissed Hoodwink on the cheek, through the balaclava. "Thank you. You're saving me by doing this. You're saving us all."

"I doubt it." He stared at her through the goggles. "But I'll do my best. I will." He wrapped his gloved fingers tentatively around the rope.

"Hoodwink?" Ari said, a hint of urgency in her tone.

"Yes?"

"Don't forget what you told me." She was blinking a little more than was usual. "Don't you ever forget it."

He was confused. "What did I say?"

"That you're coming back!" She sounded exasperated.

Hoodwink nodded carefully. "I haven't forgotten that, don't you worry." He could never forget that. He forced a smile. "I'll return. I promise. If I have to crawl through the pit of hell to do it, I'll come back for you. I swear it."

Ari's lips were trembling. She turned away to hide her face from him.

Hoodwink braced his boots against the Gate and began the long climb into eternity.

CHAPTER NINE

Hoodwink walked the rocky surface, raising himself hand-over-hand along the rope. He hadn't known what to expect, but this wasn't so bad. "Aid climbing," the Users had called it—rope laid over a route to make it easier for future climbers. He couldn't imagine what those first two climbers must have gone through to place the rope.

The climb proved a little monotonous. It was somewhat similar to trudging on the ground, bent-over, gripping a rope for balance. He understood now what it felt like to be a crooked old man like Leader. Except Leader was only twenty-nine, prematurely aged by the power that flowed through him. The same future awaited Hoodwink and his daughter. Well, whether or not he'd see that future was the question, wasn't it? He had to make it past the next few hours to start with.

The first rope went by easily enough. Hand over hand, foot over foot. Thirty minutes or so transpired.

The second rope came into view. It overlapped the first rope by some paces, so that Hoodwink could've switched or used both of them if he wanted. The first rope ended in an anchor of small cords that passed through metallic loops wedged into the stone wall.

One segment down. Nine more to go.

He bounce-tested the second cord with a quick pull, and when he felt the faint answering vibration, he slowly transferred his weight until the rope carried his entire body.

He climbed onward, hesitant at first, and then faster as his confidence grew. He was growing tired, true, but he covered the second segment almost as vigorously as the first.

He started slowing down on the third rope, when the climb began to wear on him. The rock face became at times encrusted in ice, for which the spikes on the crampons proved especially suited, the sharp metal points digging right into the ice so that the tips of his boots found purchase.

By the fourth rope, he felt like going back. His shoulders ached. His biceps throbbed. The sides of his back behind his armpits felt numb. The warmth he had felt in those down-feather clothes was long gone, so much so that his extremities throbbed painfully from the cold. He released small spurts of electricity into his fingers and toes to warm himself, knowing that he had to be careful not to exhaust his charge.

By the fifth rope, he was thoroughly beaten. He couldn't go on. By his reckoning, he'd been climbing at least three hours. But he forced himself. He promised that he would stop for a rest at the sixth.

At last, rope number six came into view, and he climbed until he reached it. He took his promised rest.

Feeling utterly spent, he knelt against the rockface, and, keeping one hand firmly on rope number five, he reached the other hand behind his lower back and grabbed rope number six. He threaded the end of number six around his waist and tied it in a knot, a tricky task with one hand—especially a gloved hand at that—but he eventually managed after slipping open the fingertips of the glove and braving the numbing wind.

He tentatively released his hold on rope number five, and when he was satisfied that the knot on number six would hold at his waist, he rested. He resealed his glove, and balled his hands to warm his fingers. He released a trickle of electricity into his extremities, and it was enough to improve the blood flow to his fingers and toes and prevent frostbite. He moved very slowly the whole time. He wanted to eat some of the salted meat from his duffel bag, but then he'd have to lift the balaclava and expose his face. Also, he was afraid that any movement would cause him to fall, which is why he kept his knees braced firmly against the rockface the whole time, unable to shake off the feeling that the rope at his waist would unravel any second.

The urge to look down proved almost overwhelming. Just one peek. What was the worst that could happen?

He'd lose heart, that's what. Not to mention the vertigo would probably overwhelm him. The same vertigo he felt if he looked up too far, and saw the hopeless, infinite grade above. By focusing on the icy rockface before him and nothing else, he made the climb doable. And by not knowing how far he'd plummet, by pretending he was only a few feet off the ground, well, that helped calm nerves that would otherwise paralyze him, or lead to a fall.

But while he didn't look down, he didn't

climb up either.

He just stayed there, gloves gently wrapped around rope number six in case the knot unraveled.

He stayed there, waiting, listening to the howling wind.

For what?

Resting, he told himself.

He was cold. So cold. It would only grow colder the higher he went. Another incentive to just stay here a little longer.

Halfway. Come on Hood. You're halfway there.

He sighed, got a good grip on the sixth rope with one hand, and reluctantly untied the knot at his waist with the other. He felt the sudden pull as his arm was forced to bear the weight of his body once more. He quickly joined his other hand to the rope, and properly placed his feet to share the load.

He jerked himself up the rope, one hand and foot at a time, his body rebelling with every step. Resting had proven a mistake because he just wanted to stop again. His muscles ached all over. He had no energy. He wasn't a climber. What was he doing out here on the Forever Gate, a mile above the city?

Saving Ari, that's what. Now climb damn it.

He climbed, not daring to overthink his motivation, knowing how easily he could poke holes in it. He climbed for Ari, and that was good enough.

Each handspan became a small battle. Though it was a battle he was determined to win.

The air became thin, and he found himself

panting constantly now. Or was he just tired?

Somehow, he reached rope number seven.

Then rope number eight.

The frigid wind tore into him incessantly, and at times it felt like he wasn't even wearing a jacket. Despite the gloves, the gusts bit into his fingers. His toes were numb inside his boots, as were his cheeks under the balaclava. He had to constantly expend some of his charge just to keep the frostbite at bay.

Finally he reached rope number nine. Whereas all the previous ropes had overlapped to some extent, the ninth rope lay *above* the eighth.

But it was only a little ways above, just an arm-length. He could handle an arm-length of bare wall, couldn't he?

He climbed to the very top of rope number eight, wrapping his hands around the metallic loops that anchored the rope into the wall. There was no ice here, just pure, unadulterated stone.

He considered opening the tips of the gloves, but then decided against it. Instead he reached up and ran the fingers of one hand along the surface, searching for something that could take his weight. There. The base of a tiny fissure. He found a higher foothold for his boot, letting the jagged crampons grab hold of the rock, and then he slowly transferred his weight to the handhold. The first joint of his finger flared in protest, but he found another foothold with his other leg, and he was able to haul himself high enough to grab the next rope.

When both his hands were secure around that rope, he exhaled in relief. He'd done it.

The ninth rope was in hand. After this, there was only one more rope to go.

He climbed mechanically now more than anything else. Raise one hand. Then the other. Raise one foot. Then the other. His arms and legs felt like stones. He thought they'd drop off if he stopped. He kept his focus on the wall in front of him at all times.

Raise one hand. Then the other.

And then it was done. He arrived at the loops and cords that anchored rope number nine, and he glanced upward, searching for the final rope.

He saw only the dizzying Forever Gate, reaching skyward in unending infinity.

He had reached the Death Zone, where every moment counted.

And there was no tenth rope.

Worse, it had started to snow.

CHAPTER TEN

What is a mind?

Why does it betray us at those times when we need it most?

Why does it fill us with fear, and emotion, at those times when we most need to avoid fear, when we most need to be emotionless?

Perhaps the better question might be, what is reality?

Is it some cog in a giant wheel? A smaller part of a grander fabrication, of which we all play our bit parts? Are our lives merely parts of this wheel? Predetermined and preset? We live out our days, and time passes, inexorably, slowly building up to one key, quintessential climax, where all the choices we think we've made and the paths we think we've taken converge beyond our control, and we find ourselves on a rope along a wall miles above the city we were born in. At the Death Zone, with another quarter-mile to go.

And that rope has just run out.

Hoodwink leaned his head against the rockface, and closed his eyes.

It was over. He'd have to climb all the way back down. He'd have to tell Ari he couldn't do it.

The rope had run out, he'd say. *The rope had run out.*

And he could see her, looking back at him with disappointment in her eyes as she set out to climb the wall in his place. *I wouldn't have needed a rope,* she'd say.

Hoodwink opened his eyes, and he did what he'd promised himself he wouldn't do.

He looked down.

The city looked almost unreal at this height. It was like he stood again beside the street vendor with her miniature replicas and maps again, and casually observed one of her wares. True, this was far more detailed than any map he'd ever seen, but the illusion of perception made the city seem much closer through the goggles, like he could just reach out and pick it up.

But then his eyes focused on the whirling snow closer at hand, those flakes descending from the heights like an endless vortex of doom, and the reality of what he saw hit him. He felt suddenly nauseous, and dizzy.

The duffel bag abruptly slid down his shoulder. He let go of the rope with that hand and caught the bag in the crook of his forearm. Two bundles of salted meat tumbled free and spun away on the breeze as the upper winds picked them up. Entranced, he watched the bundles fall. The fingers of the hand that gripped the rope began to slip. It would be so easy to follow those bundles down...

He snapped his head away, slid the duffel bag back into place, and placed both hands firmly on the rope. He concentrated on the bare rockface just ahead.

I can climb without a rope. I can climb without a rope. I can climb...

Could he really?

It was cold. So damn cold. The dead of winter in the coldest of winters yet, and he lay miles up from the earth. The snow fell more heavily. If this kept up, he doubted he'd be able to see farther than a pace or two. And the sun would set soon. If he was caught on the wall in the dark, he'd freeze to death.

Yes. Better to go back now, while he still could. He couldn't climb this. That howling wind would either freeze him to the bone, or tear him from the rock. Or the lack of oxygen in the Death Zone would take him. He wasn't trained for this. He was thirty-five years old. Sure, he was fit because of his job building barrels, but hammering nails into wood was far different than pulling one's body up a rockface.

He had to go back.

He had to admit when defeat had slapped him in the face.

Just like how he'd admitted defeat when Jeremy and the gols took away his daughter. Just like how he'd given up and buried himself in his job, and spent the nights in the tavern, going home miserably drunk, and hating himself. *Hating*. He'd *wanted* his wife to leave him. He'd wanted to be punished, for allowing his daughter to be taken. Every morning he'd passed Ari by on the way to work, and he'd never said a word. He'd given up. Like he gave up now.

He had a rare moment of absolute lucidity right then.

The rockface wasn't his enemy.

It never had been.

It was cliche to think it, but *he* was his most ruthless enemy. *He* was the one he had to fight.

He could climb this wall.

And he *would*.

He was through giving up.

He shut his eyes, and breathed deeply, remembering why he was doing this.

I won't let you die Ari.

Opening his eyes, he flipped open the fingertips of both gloves by sliding them one at a time against the rope. The wind assailed his numb fingers, but he let a small spark of electricity flow into them, warming the flesh.

Before he could change his mind he let one hand leave the rope. He felt along the rough surface with his bare fingers, seeking a handhold. There. He forced his fingers into a slight crevice, and raised a boot, wedging the crampons into a foothold. He pulled with his arm and leg at the same time, and flinched as the finger joints bore the weight of his body.

He planted the opposite boot on a small ledge, and straightened the leg, reaching up to find a handhold for the corresponding arm. He squeezed his fingers onto a tiny shelf, and paused for an instant.

The only thing holding him up was the strength of his own body. There was no rope. No second-chances should he make a mistake. He rode death's horse by the tips of his fingers and the tips of his toes.

He tried not to think about that for too long.

Focus, Hood.

The fingers of both hands throbbed at their first joints, but it was a manageable pain.

He lifted his knee, planted his boot on a new foothold, and pressed upward. His torso rose, and he scrambled the fingers of one hand along the wall, searching for a handhold.

But before he could find that handhold, the newly-placed foot slipped, the crampons breaking away a small section of the wall.

Hoodwink slammed against the rock and his other boot lost footing. He hung there by one hand, the finger joints bearing the brunt of his weight. Only the tensile strength of a couple of knuckles stood between him and oblivion. Knuckles that throbbed in torment.

He scrambled with his left hand along the rockface, searching for a hold, any hold. Incredibly, he couldn't find one. Nothing would support him. A tiny ledge there. Too slippery. A crevice here. His fingers wouldn't fit.

The knuckles of his other hand had held thus far, but it was the arm muscles that now started to fail. His entire arm shook uncontrollably.

Frantically, he lifted his forgotten feet. He had to find a foothold.

There. A small jutting piece of rock. Just a fragment. But he was able to jam the spikes of both boots onto it, sharing the weight with his arm. The pain in his knuckles subsided a little, but the arm was still shaking rapidly, near exhaustion. He searched the wall again with his free hand, finding a hold he'd missed the first time, and trusted his weight to it.

Carefully, he released the first shaking hand from the wall. His fingers were curled into a permanent claw, and he found himself unable to straighten them through the pain.

He allowed more electricity into the hand, massaging the tendons and bone with that spark, worried that he'd never be able to open his hand again. With an effort he was finally able to coax each finger open.

He reached up, found the next handhold, and had to curl up those sore fingers all over again.

In this way he proceeded up the last section of the wall, battling against himself, battling against the rock. First one foot, then one hand. Then the other hand. Then the other foot. Rising one small handspan at a time. Conquering infinity bit by bit. Warming his extremities with electricity.

He came to a section of rock that was covered in ice. He extended an arm and searched with his bare fingertips, seeking a handhold. His fingers slipped everywhere he placed them, and he couldn't find a grip. He was beginning to despair when he remembered the two ice axes he had stowed away in the duffel bag.

This would be a tricky maneuver. He carefully opened the drawstring of his duffel bag with one hand, and then groped inside until he found both ice axes. He made sure they were side by side, and oriented the same way, and then he wrapped his fingers around the handles and delicately slid the axes out. He reached up, and slammed both axes into the ice above him. The serrated picks dug deep. He pulled on the handles, testing the hold. It seemed firm enough. Shifting his weight to the axes, he released his other arm from the wall and grabbed the leftmost ax so that he held one handle in each palm now. He released the rightmost ax momentarily to pull the drawstring and shut the duffel bag.

He proceeded up the frozen layer, striking the wall with the ice axes, letting the picks find a hold. The crampons on his boots proved their worth here, allowing him to easily pierce the ice and make his own footholds. All in all, the going was actually much easier than when he had to pull himself up by his fingertips alone. His only worry as he climbed was that an entire sheet of ice would break away while he was on it, perhaps caused by the very motion of striking the wall with the picks. But he compelled himself onward nonetheless, winning countless small battles, not backing down from adversity.

It's not real, he told himself often during that climb. *None of this is real.* A part of him even believed it. Some other world existed atop his own, one that he couldn't see, couldn't feel, but was there nonetheless, where he resided at the same time as this one. And it was from that other world, that other self, from which he drew his strength and focus.

It's not real.

Tiny bits of matter called muscle rubbed against each other, powered by a mind comprised of similar tiny bits. This muscle manipulated tiny bits of matter called axes, which in turn struck tiny bits of matter that formed ice. All of those tiny bits made the fiction called reality. Spitting in the face of this reality, denying that it and his own mortality even existed, that's what kept him going.

Warmed by the electricity of vitra, he climbed, constantly reminded that there was no rope supporting him. That the only thing keeping him from the long fingers of oblivion was his own intensity of will. It was strange, having death so close to him in that climb. He'd never felt such clarity. He'd never felt so full of life.

He'd never felt so free.

And then it was done. One moment he was his raising hands and feet with all the intensity of his will and focus, and the next he was pulling himself onto the wall's upper lip, a ledge little wider than his waist. He cleared away a small layer of snow and settled himself onto the ledge.

It came as sort of a shock to have actually made it. Here he was, in a snowstorm at the top of the world, the frigid gusts whipping his hood, and he'd just climbed the last leg of the Forever Gate without a rope.

He held out his arms, raising the ice axes, and loosed a shout of victory that was lost in the wind. A few tears spilled from his eyes, and he felt the droplets solidify against the bottom edge of his goggles.

He crouched down against the rim of the Gate, utterly exhausted. He peered down the other side of the wall, wondering what wonders or horrors lay beyond the Forever Gate.

But the white-out of the snowstorm veiled the landscape below.

Of course.

It was with more than a little relief that he

spotted the rope that led down into the depths a short way to his left. He couldn't see where the rope anchored—the top was covered in snow and ice from the ledge. But that didn't matter. The hard work was done and he had a way down.

For now he needed a moment's rest.

He remained where he was, staring over the ledge into eternity, at the downward vortex of windswept snow.

He'd never felt so drained in his life. The sheer intensity of focus needed to climb that wall had drained him to the core. So he just stayed there on the wall, letting the snow fall around him, and the wind pick at his bones.

He lay back, and his eyes drifted shut.

He started to fall asleep.

He heard Leader's voice at the back of his mind.

You'll feel utterly exhausted because of the thin air. You won't be able to think clearly. You'll want to fall asleep. But fall asleep and you die.

He batted the voice away. A short nap wouldn't hurt anything. Besides, dying didn't sound half bad right about now. It would be an end to this incredible weariness at least.

Fall asleep and YOU DIE.

He forced himself upright.

He refused to die now, after all this work. He *refused.*

Using the ice axes and the spikes at the tips of his boots, he pulled himself along the icy ledge in kind of hunched crawl, making his way toward the rope that led down the other side. He was about to swing himself onto that rope when he remembered he was supposed to update the Users on his progress. He could imagine Ari sitting by the twin of the rigged diary he carried, staring at the blank pages, anxiously awaiting word of his progress.

But maybe he was just feeding his fatherly ego. Did she even care about him? She said he wasn't her father anymore. She was right. All that she was had been destroyed with her revisal. She had memories of a different father. Memories of another man bringing her to the market square every weekend. Memories of another father comforting her when she fell from the sleigh and hurt herself.

She wasn't his little girl anymore.

No, that wasn't true. No matter what memories she had, she *was* his little girl.

He set himself firmly on the ledge and resolutely slid off the duffel bag from his shoulder. He retrieved the diary.

It was an ordinary seeming book. For all he knew, it had no magical properties whatsoever, and any messages he printed here would remain here. He just had to trust in Leader's word, he supposed.

He slid the writing stylus from its clip on the book's spine, and pressed it to the page. He had to hold the pages down in the wind as he wrote.

I've made the top of the Gate, he transcribed. His script was terrible. He could barely grip the pencil after a climb like that, and the numbing cold didn't help, even though he sent a surge of electricity through his joints. This entry would have to be short. *Snowstorm hides other side. Climbing down now.*

There. That should do.

He started to return the diary to the duffel bag when a gust of wind snatched the book from him. He fumbled for the thing—

But it was too late, and the book plunged over the ledge.

He watched the diary spiral away into the vortex, soon vanishing in the snowstorm.

With a sigh, Hoodwink stowed the ice picks in the duffel bag and secured the bag to his shoulder. Then he lowered himself onto the rope and began the long climb down the other side.

The descent proved much faster than the ascent. He rappelled down the wall, using the existing ropes left by the previous climbers. All of those ropes seemed to be intact this time. Even so, the way was frigid, and he was forced to expend his charge keeping warm on the way down.

When at last he reached the bottom, he was exhausted, and his charge was spent. He set foot on strangely soft ground, and instantly the snowstorm lifted.

He turned away from the wall to face a world entirely unlike the one he had left behind...

CHAPTER ELEVEN

Hoodwink stood in a desert. Sand dunes stretched to the horizon, unbroken by any landmarks. Though it had been evening at the top of the Gate, time had reset, and the sun stood in the midpoint of the sky. The wall of the Forever Gate behind Hoodwink was the only landmark of note, unless you counted the bones of giant beasts in the distance, half-buried in the sand. The skeletons of monsters from the nine hells?

Despite the desert dunes and the bright sun, he still felt frigid, and his breath fogged white as ever. Yet when he took one step away from the wall, the heat swelled over him in waves, hotter and stronger than he'd ever felt it. He retreated against the wall, and the freezing cold enveloped him once more.

Shaking his head in disbelief, he steeled himself and then stepped forward. It felt like he'd stepped into an oven.

He untied and lowered his hood. He took off his goggles. He pulled the balaclava from his head, then knelt and unbuckled the crampons from his boots. He stripped off the remainder of his winter clothes, taking the dagger from the jacket's inner pocket and stuffing it into his trousers. He abandoned the clothes and the steel spikes at the base of the Forever Gate—there was simply no room for them in the small duffel bag.

He advanced, swilling water from the frozen bladder stowed in the duffel bag. The ice inside melted slowly, drip-feeding him the liquid.

The sand swallowed him past the ankles with each step, and he could feel the heat of the dunes through his boots. The molten sun beat down mercilessly.

He wasn't sure how long he marched, because the sun didn't seem to be moving in the sky. He guessed an hour. Long enough for the contents of the water bladder to melt entirely, anyway. And for him to drink it all.

He paused in the shade of one of those leviathans of bone. The unburied portion of the skull proved colossal, and comprised the greater proportion of the thing. From the skull extended the backbone, to which a prodigious basket of ribs was attached, erupting from the sand like a giant claw. The middle ribs had the greatest arch—bigger than some of the city footbridges. The backbone tapered as it continued toward the tail, which fanned outward in a massive rake.

He ran his fingertips across the surface of one of those ribs. The bone was porous, and had a similar texture to the Gate he had just climbed. The macabre notion came to him that the Forever Gate might be made of the bones of these beasts.

His tread became slower as time inched by and the heat sapped him. With the water bladder empty, his lips became hopelessly chapped, and his throat felt swollen. Yet he trudged aimlessly onward. There was nowhere else to go but forward. He estimated that half a day had passed since he began, yet the sun still hadn't moved a fingerbreadth in the sky.

He decided he'd take shelter in the shadow of the next giant skeleton he found. Ahead, off to the right, a suitable candidate awaited.

But before he reached the leviathan, he unexpectedly ran up against a glass barrier, flattening his face against its surface.

He slid a sweaty hand along the glass, his fingers making a distinct squeegee sound. On a whim he slammed a hand into it. The surface thudded as if it were made of thick stone. He retrieved the dagger from his trousers and slammed the hilt into the glass with both hands. THUD. This time a vibration passed along the surface. He plunged the dagger into the surface next, but the blade skidded and twisted his wrist at a painful angle. The resultant sound he heard from the barrier reminded him of pebbles skimming along ice.

He held up a palm and summoned as much electricity as he was able, but only a trickle remained, and the tendrils of energy sparked harmlessly across the surface.

Then he noticed the hooded figure standing beside the glass, not far from him. Dressed in a black gown, the figure held a scythe in its hand.

Hoodwink spun toward the figure, dagger raised. "Who are you?"

The figure said no words, but it advanced, extending a hand that was much like the bony tails of those leviathans Hoodwink had passed. The hem of the figure's robe remained stationary, as if the thing floated rather than walked. It left no footprints in the sand.

"Stay back!" Hoodwink rasped, keeping his

dagger aimed high. Of all times to have no charge...

He retreated and his right elbow skidded against the glass barrier. He lost his balance, falling to the sand.

He swiveled toward the figure—

But it was gone.

"A mirage." Hoodwink laughed a laugh that quickly became a dry cough.

"Not entirely," came a quaint voice beside him.

Still on the ground, Hoodwink spun his dagger on the new arrival. It was a dwarf, dressed in a leather jerkin and breeches, with openwork sandals around his hairy toes. The dwarf held a black umbrella, which he put to use shading his head. The symbol on his chest suggested he was a gol, though Hoodwink didn't recognize the occupation the symbol stood for. It was either three vertical lines, or the number one hundred eleven.

"Think of the image of Death as a test," the dwarf said. "You failed."

"Who are you?" Hoodwink said, unable to hold back another cough.

"Here." The dwarf popped the cork from a fresh water bladder, and tossed it to Hoodwink. "You sound terrible."

Hoodwink caught the bladder and eyed the lip suspiciously. He smelled it and then took a sip. Water. Sweet water. He drank voraciously, finally setting the bladder down with a sigh and wiping his lips.

"Better?" the dwarf said. "Good. Now we can talk about what we're going to do with you."

Hoodwink scrambled upright, using the glass barrier as a lever for his weary body. He kept the dagger pointed at the dwarf. "Who are you?"

"I am Seven," the dwarf said. "One of the main A.I.s of the system."

"The main what?" Hoodwink stared blankly at the dwarf.

"The Artificial Intelligences. One of the Master Golems, if you will."

"I *knew* you were a gol." Hoodwink glanced around uncertainly, wondering if any more approached in ambush. He saw only the empty desert.

"I'm very much alone," Seven said. "In more ways than you know."

"Well, I'm Hoodwink. Hoodwink Cooper. And I have a message for you gols out here."

"Oh?" Seven raised an eyebrow.

"John Baker," Hoodwink said. "Son of Arrold Baker, 18 Market Street."

Seven pursed his lips. "Yes?"

"You're to get in touch with him. He's your contact for the Users, he is. We want to help you, if we can."

Seven seemed genuinely puzzled now. "The closest city would be Section 9, and my backup copy of the records shows a house on 18 Market Street. But what is it exactly the Users want to help me with?"

"The sickness that's affecting the minds of you gols." When Seven stared back blankly, Hoodwink elaborated. "The slobbering faces. The mistakes made by the gols at the banks, the stores, and so forth. You gols aren't yourselves. Not that I care, of course. You could all die as far as I'm concerned. But I'm just the messenger."

Understanding seemed to dawn on the dwarf. "I see now. But unfortunately, there's a slight problem. I've lost communication with the Core. The Attack has damaged the root fiber and I can't interact with my complementary units. I'm afraid if you want to convey this message of yours, you'll have to travel through the Forever Gate and do it yourself."

Hoodwink narrowed his eyes. "What are you talking about? I just crossed the Gate."

"What you refer to as the 'Forever Gate' is just an artifice, a wall used to keep the humans from eating up all our computational resources. It would take googols more processing power if we allowed you beyond the towns. Generating fractal terrain doesn't come cheap, you know. Throw in the particle system, the billboarding, the occlusion culling, not to mention the lightmapping and pathfinding, all of which need to be duplicated for each and every city, and you have a system whose resources are quite nearly spent. It's a miracle it all comes together as smoothly as it does, really."

Hoodwink waved his dagger threateningly. "Speak Common, will you?"

Seven smiled, and there actually seemed to be irony, real irony in those gol eyes. "You've been hoodwinked."

Hoodwink stared at the dwarf, not knowing what to say. Then he had a thought. He indicated the glass barrier beside him, and rapped the surface with his knuckles. "This is the true Forever Gate, isn't it? The real world, the one you've been hiding from us, it's past here."

Seven pursed his lips, then nodded, a little reluctantly. "You could say that."

"Tell me how to cross."

"If you cross the Forever Gate, there's no coming back," Seven said.

Hoodwink felt a tingle of dread in the pit of his stomach, but he said, "I've heard that before. And I will come back."

"We'll see. You needn't have come all this way simply to pass the Forever Gate. Because you see, it can be crossed by anyone, anywhere."

Hoodwink regarded the dwarf doubtfully. "Really? Enlighten me."

Seven extended his arms and smiled mockingly. "Take your dagger, wedge it in the sand, and fall on it."

Hoodwink stared at the dwarf, feeling his anger rise.

"It's true," Seven said. "Dying is the only way to reach the Outside. It's in the programming. Those who sent you over the wall, these Users, they likely hoped you'd fall to your death during the climb."

Hoodwink considered this for a moment. Then a smile crept on his face.

"You're a malicious, conniving little gol aren't you?" Hoodwink said. "I don't think I've ever met one quite like you. Except, I'm not so gullible as you might think, I'm not. You may've tricked the others who came before me, but you won't take me so easily."

The dwarf spread his hands wider. "I have sold you the only real truth there is."

"You sell death!" Hoodwink said.

"But isn't death the final truth?" Seven turned around, and began walking in the opposite direction. He glanced over his shoulder. "The Forever Gate *is* death. Either cross death and deliver your message, or return to the city, change your name, and your face, and live out your life. And get yourself collared again if you want that life to be long."

"Don't you turn your back on me." Hoodwink rushed at the dwarf with the dagger, unleashing a guttural growl.

But the dwarf turned around and his fingertips glowed with forks of lightning. The brunt of the bolt swept past Hoodwink, but he was sent flying into the glass barrier by the trailing electrical tendrils. Sparks pulsed away from his body in surges that were absorbed into the glass as he slid to the ground.

"The next blow will not be so gentle," Seven said.

"Impossible," Hoodwink panted. He cringed at the pain he felt in his side. Broken ribs, or worse. "Gols don't have that power. It's why you collar us."

"Has anything you've seen today been possible?" the dwarf said. "Return to the city and live out your life. I'll see you on the Outside when you're good and ready."

Hoodwink noticed a flicker from the corner of his eye. Seven's lightning had done something to the glass barrier. Where the main bolt had struck, the glass intermittently faded in and out, going from a view of the desert beyond to a triangular gap of darkness the size of a man, and back again.

Seven followed his gaze, but said nothing.

Hoodwink stood, and lifted his dagger toward the defect in the glass. He touched the gap. The tip of the weapon vanished. Although the view alternated from darkness to dunes and back again, the weapon appeared in neither. It was like he held only a clipped hilt.

When he pulled the weapon out, the dagger was whole.

"You have found your Forever Gate after all," Seven said. "Stepping beyond the outermost boundaries of the system is the same as death."

"As I said, I'm not so gullible." The dagger had returned. He would too.

He hoped.

He glanced at Seven. "Better pray I don't find you on the other side."

Before he could change his mind—and he was very close to changing it—Hoodwink stepped through the gap.

CHAPTER TWELVE

The world deflated like a child's balloon.

Hoodwink awoke in some kind of goo. He couldn't open his eyelids, because the substance burned his eyes. He couldn't breathe, because his lungs were filled with the stuff. He kicked and writhed, and in his panic he discovered a pliant membrane. He pressed on it with his hands, and it enveloped his arms up to the elbows. Abruptly the sheath yielded, and he slid into the open air.

He landed on a hard floor, the goo splattering all around him. He thrashed, coughing the fluid from his lungs, spitting the mucoidal substance from his mouth. He scooped the goo from his eye sockets, and he was able to open his lids for short spurts, though his eyes still burned, and he saw flashes of an iron hallway.

As his cough subsided, and the air flowed in and out of his lungs, he devoted more time to clearing the goo from his eyes. He blinked rapidly, letting the tears flow, and he was able to open the lids for longer and longer periods. His right eyelid had a bit of a painful tic, but he ignored it.

A rotating red light mounted near the pod bathed the scene alternately in shadow and light. He was lying on an iron grill. There was a siren wailing.

He forced himself to sit upright. A strange weight pressed into his gut.

He glanced down.

An umbilical cord was attached to his belly.

Pulsating blue veins ran down its surface.

A sudden repugnance overcame him and he pulled frantically at the cord. Pain flashed through his insides, and he immediately let go of the thing. The opposite end was still buried somewhere inside the pod he'd emerged from, so he grabbed the cord in the middle and yanked. He had to put most of his body weight into the act, but finally the cord slurped from the pod with a loud "pop." The placental end slapped his cheek, and he tossed the gory tissue away in disgust.

He attempted to stand, but his feet refused to obey. His eyes were drawn to the scrawny limbs that made up his legs. His muscle had vanished. His legs were just skin stretched over bone, the knobby shapes of his knees the only indication that these even *were* legs. His arms fared little better, thin pipes of skin and bone.

What had the Gate done to him?

He tried to access the power inside him, but the spark didn't exist anymore. It was as if that part of his mind had been snipped away.

He was filled with a sudden sense of urgency. He had to get away from this place.

He dragged himself ever so slowly along the iron grill that was the floor, using the gaps for purchase, the beacon lighting the way in swathes of red and black, the siren keening. The wasted muscles in his arms and legs screamed in constant protest. It was like climbing the last leg of the Forever Gate all over again. Inch-by-inch he crawled, like the lowest of worms, the umbilical cord dragging along behind him. He kept his lower body tilted to the side, and he was careful not to put too much weight on the tender section of his belly where the cord still attached.

He paused when he realized there were more pods like the one he'd just left behind lining either side of the wall. The membranes were slightly translucent, and he could see human forms floating in each with the umbilical cords still attached. Through the floor grill below he perceived another level of pods. And above him, past the ceiling grill, still another level with more pods.

Pods upon pods upon pods.

A doorway in the rightmost wall opened onto a massive room. He crawled forward, onto a balcony of sorts, and stared through the grill at the strange activity below.

Mechanical monstrosities were at work, though at what they labored he had no idea. They moved pincers to and fro above compartments that spilled long threads of different colors. Below them, the metal floor was blackened in several places, as though the area had suffered recent fire.

The siren wailed on.

There was a flash, and he heard a loud boom. The hall shook. He glanced upward. The ceiling was a dome made of glass, or so he thought, because he could see the night sky beyond. But this was not the night sky he was used to—a large, multicolored ball floated amid the stars, about the size of his fist when held at arm's-length. Amid the chaos of colors in that ball, he noticed a pattern near the lower right that was eerily similar to a human eye. It was Jupiter, he realized. A planet he'd seen in books.

Another flash. Another boom. The floor shook, and cracks spidered across the glass dome.

"Warning," a female voice droned. "Decompression imminent. Warning. Decompression imminent."

He heard a whir behind him. One of those mechanical monstrosities had rolled onto the balcony from the hall he'd left. In place of legs it had treads. In place of arms, pincers. Its body was a barrel of steel. Its head looked similar to the hilt of a sword, with curved cross-guards and a central haft. Three glass disks stared back at him from the depths of that hilt, and a red light floated above the center disk.

The thing wrapped a set of pincers around his leg and dragged him back into the corridor. The monstrosity hauled him through that hallway of pods. The world shook, and he heard a distant boom, but the monstrosity did not cease.

The thing finally turned into another room, and lifted him dangling by the foot over a strange moving floor as if to dump him.

"Wait!" Hoodwink said.

The monstrosity paused, lifting him so that his upside-down head was at the same level as those glass eyes.

"John Baker," Hoodwink said. He slurred the words, like someone who knew how to talk, but had never used his tongue and lips. "Son of Arrold Baker, 18 Market Street." What was that the dwarf had called his city? "9th section. John Baker. The Users want to help. Meet John Baker."

He thought he saw an iris in each of those three glass disks enlarge, as if the monstrosity considered his words, then its head tilted up once, and then down. A conscious expression of agreement? Or the mechanical equivalent of a nervous tic?

The monstrosity unceremoniously hurled him onto the sliding surface, then wheeled about and left.

The moving floor was soft compared to the previous one. And slightly pliable. His stomach tightened when he saw that he had company. But it wasn't the kind of company anyone would want. Two human bodies lay not far from him, pale bodies crimped in death. Burned.

His face felt suddenly hot. With his eyes, he followed the motion of the floor to its destination—some kind of grinder. He could hear the terrible whirr from here, and see the fountain of blood as one of the dead fell inside.

He groped frantically along the rolling surface, pulling himself toward the edge.

But he had only seconds.

Not enough time.

Before the grinder took him, his last thoughts were of Ari.

He'd done it. He'd delivered the message. He'd saved her.

Yet the victory was bittersweet, because he'd broken his final promise.

Guess I won't be coming back.

The grinder swallowed him.

CHAPTER THIRTEEN

Hoodwink awoke.

He floated in water, like in the dream.

He could see in all directions at once, like in the dream.

360-degrees of horror.

Small particles passed in and out of his flesh. His hands were tentacles. His legs, suckers. His torso, a bell-shaped, glowing mass. He had a tail. Fleshy cords moored him in place.

Around him floated other forms just like him, secured in place by similar moorings to long, horizontal tubes. Their bodies glowed, a thousand forms giving light to the otherwise lightless waters.

A telepathic message voiced in his mind then, a rapid series of moans and clicks that he shouldn't have understood, but he did.

Welcome to the real world, Hoodwink

He screamed.

SPECIAL SNEAK PREVIEW

The following pages contain a brief excerpt from

The

Forever

Gate II

the second book in Isaac Hooke's *Forever Gate* saga.

Coming January 2013.

Ari sat by the frosty window, and sipped rosemary tea with shaking hands. She stared at the snow-covered street outside, and contemplated a life that was nearing its end.

She was only twenty-nine years old, though she looked ninety-nine. Vitra had ravaged her body, sucked away her youth, leaving a shriveled shell. Like all Users, she was destined to flare blindingly bright in life, only to burn out all too soon.

Ten years had passed since Hoodwink had gone. Somehow he'd gotten his message through. Somehow he'd passed the Forever Gate and communicated with the gols. He'd become legendary among the Users for it.

But the contact had proven disastrous. The gols used the opportunity to lay a trap, and almost every last User had died. Only Ari and Leader survived.

She was Leader now. In those ten years, she'd relaunched the group, and given everything she had to them. Body. Mind. *Soul.* For what? It hadn't mattered. She hadn't changed a thing. The world was still dying and there was nothing she could do about it. The snowstorms worsened, the cold became colder. More and more of the gols fell victim to the mind plague. And then there was The Drop, a relatively recent phenomenon that involved human beings dropping dead for no apparent reason. Not just one at a time, mind, but hundreds throughout the city. Men, women and children. Young and old. It didn't matter who you were, or what you were doing, you weren't immune to The Drop. If you don't watch out, The Drop's going to get you. Don't do any wrong, or The Drop'll have ya. The Drop. The Drop. The Drop.

Society was falling apart. Despite her best efforts. Despite her attempts to seize power from Jeremy, the mayor. Jeremy. She'd had to leave him, seven years ago, when it became too obvious she was a User, and aging at a rate far faster than normal. Jeremy probably wasn't all that happy, given how much he'd paid to have the gols revise her against her will. Then again, he'd taken another wife soon after, so maybe he was glad Ari left. Glad to replace her with a young, beautiful wife.

Beauty. It'd been a curse, in her youth. Suitors had pursued her relentlessly, never granting her peace. Jeremy had protected her through it all, and only he won her heart in the end. He was—no, those were false memories. Just as most of her personality had been false, fashioned specifically for the marriage. Her knowledge of poetry, music, and painting. Her comprehension of politics, social intelligence, and manipulation. Her skills in the bedroom. She was programmed to be his perfect mate.

Only her political talents were still of some use. The remaining skills? Utter chaff. She had no piano to play. No canvas to paint. No one cared about her poetry. And no one would make love to her.

She was alone in this tiny shack of a house, which was a pittance compared to the luxury she was used to, and her only contact with the outside world was through the furtive missives sent to the New Users. That and the human nurse who visited once a day to bathe her and prepare her meals. Sometimes she confused him for Jeremy, and even addressed him "Mayor." The nurse always humored her, saying "yes Ari" to most everything she said. Because of that, occasionally she played tricks on him, or told him terrible swear words involving her most intimate body parts to see how he'd react, but the response was always the same. "Yes Ari."

She set down her cup angrily. *Yes Ari.* How she despised that patronizing nurse. Didn't he understand the power she wielded? Didn't he realize that she could vaporize him with a thought? She'd grown so vast in power these past ten years. She was one of the strongest Users, despite her outward appearance, and vitra literally stormed within her.

Her tea had grown cold. She allowed electricity to spark from her fingers, and instantly the liquid boiled. She took a tentative sip. Ah, much better. She remembered a time when hot tea scalded her tongue. These days it was the only thing she could drink—everything else felt cold. It was getting so very hard to keep warm at her age. So very hard.

But I'm not that old! a part of her shouted. All she had to do was look at the liver spots on her trembling hands. *Oh yes you are.*

A hurried knock came at the front door and she almost dropped the cup.

"I'm coming! I'm coming!" She crankily grabbed her cane, and steeled herself for what would come. She stood all at once, and flinched at the agony in her left knee. Something always hurt these days. Her left knee. Her right shoulder. Her lower back. She massaged electricity into the knee, and it helped, a little.

The knocking at the front door became more frantic.

"*I said I was coming!*" She began the long journey to the door. The shack was small, but so was her stride, and she crossed the room step by tiny step. She wondered who was bothering her this morning. The nurse wasn't scheduled to visit for another three hours.

She finally reached the door, and paused a moment, not at all looking forward to the cold that would come. The blasted fool outside the door knocked again, and she opened the door irritably.

A wave of frigid air assailed her. *Damn this cold!*

Shivering, she recognized Jackson, a messenger who'd joined the New Users a year ago. He was the highly-connected cousin of the mayor. A little on the dumb side.

"What is it?" Her breath misted. "Why have you come here in broad daylight? Were you followed?" She glanced at the snowy street behind him. There were only a few people about. Human.

"Leader Ari!" Jackson bowed excitedly.

"Yes yes." Ari waved a dismissive hand. "Spare me the formalities and answer the question damn you."

Jackson bounced on his heels rather exuberantly. "He's done it. He's really done it. He's crossed back!"

"Who's crossed back? Speak plainly, idiot!" Old age had made her a little crabby, she had to admit. That, and the irrepressible cold.

The man offered her an open journal.

Ari no longer noticed the man, nor the breath misting between them, nor even the cold. All of her attention was on that diary, which she recognized immediately. It was the diary that was twin to the one Hoodwink had taken with him, a diary rigged to instantly reflect any words written in his copy. It was the diary that was kept on display in the New User headquarters deep underground, reverently left open to the page of Hoodwink's last missive ten years ago. It was the diary she'd sat beside for weeks after he'd gone, futilely waiting for a message from her father, a message that never came.

Something new was written beneath the last entry, in Hoodwink's own handwriting. A single sentence:

Told you I'd come back.

Postpartum

If you loved this book, please consider leaving a comment on Goodreads here:

http://www.goodreads.com/book/show/17203160

Or Amazon here:

http://amzn.to/VwPNJK

(Or just search for The Forever Gate on each site)

Comments and reviews allow readers to discover indie authors, so if you want others to enjoy *The Forever Gate - Part One* as you have, don't be shy about leaving a short note!

Thanks in advance.

Keeping In Touch

You can keep in touch with me or my writing through one—or all—of the following means:

Twitter: @IsaacHooke

Facebook: http://fb.me/authorisaachooke

Goodreads: http://goodreads.com/isaachooke

My website: http://isaachooke.com

My email: isaac@isaachooke.com

Don't be shy about emails, I love getting them, and try to respond to everyone!

Thanks again for reading *The Forever Gate - Part One*, and I look forward to having you along for Part II.

WWW.ISAACHOOKE.COM

CPSIA information can be obtained at www.ICGtesting.com
Printed in the USA
LVOW11s0238030714

392724LV00026B/630/P